CAMP IRIS

WHERE ALL THE COLORS OF THE RAINBOW BELONG

CAMP IRIS

WHERE ALL THE COLORS OF THE RAINBOW BELONG

MCGEE MATHEWS

SAPPHIRE BOOKS

SALINAS, CALIFORNIA

Dedication

For Chris, who continues to amaze me with her intelligence, energy, strength, kindness, and love. She also assures me the funny parts are funny. I can't imagine these trips around the sun without you beside me.

Acknowledgement

First, I would like to thank my friend Miranda, who politely listened to my pitch for this story and laughed at the right times. Her tips on teen fashion and attitudes were most helpful. Justin helped with video suggestions and Stephanie was my expert on all things drag related. My niece Natalie shared insights into the interactions of teenagers, including attitudes on all things LGBTQ+.

I had several people reading sections/drafts for me. Carrie McWorter bravely slogged through an early draft, helping with appropriate slang for her generation. Vicki Harris was my insider for all things technical. Kim Dyke and Annette Mori both read through early drafts, even as this genre was not their typical preference.

I appreciate Sapphire Books Publishing for believing in this story. Chris and her team have once again made sure I put my best foot forward. Heather Flournoy waved her magical editing wand and the book is better for her efforts, both in content and details like spelling and my continued inability to select lay or lie. Her kind words keep many authors writing.

Thank you to the readers. Without you, there's no reason to write. I hope you enjoy my shift from my usual stories.

Chapter One
June 3

Hunched into a red-and-black gaming chair, Nikki Podolski laughed loud enough to drown out the comments of the YouTuber as he played a power washer game. It was juvenile even for her, but she found it hilarious. The alarm on her phone roared like a dinosaur. She reached over and hit silent mode. With a few clicks of her controller, the image on the screen disappeared, replaced by a brightly colored game logo. A hum blasted from the sound bar. She grabbed the remote and cut it off.

She slid her headphones on over her dishwater-blond hair and entered the lobby of the game. A voice drifted from one ear to the other. "Eagle One, come in."

Nikki adjusted the ear pads and said, "Eagle One to Sparrow."

Her friend Georgi said, "I thought I got to be a falcon now."

Nikki smiled. "Yeah, whatever. Eagle One to Raptor."

The voice cracked. "You're not taking this seriously."

"I can't. My cat is pushing me out of the chair." A plump orange cat nudged his way farther onto her lap.

"Cut back on his treats." Georgi was not a fan of cats.

In the basement of the suburban split-level,

the spacious dim room featured worn tan carpet and paneling installed before her mother was born. Its best feature was an enormous television. Ed, her stepfather, might be uninterested in updating decor, but he loved every sport imaginable. The result was a 4K TV, which Nikki currently had in game mode. She had connected two game systems, her computer, and another monitor. As long as he had a clear view from his leather recliner—and she remembered to change back to cable programming after—he didn't mind her adding her equipment. He even put in a small refrigerator between their chairs for drinks.

"Okay, I'm going in," Georgi said.

A new character popped into view.

Nikki stared at the avatar, which was clad in combat gear and a little more adult than usual. The chest was distracting, even more than the green hair. "Whoa."

"Whoa what?"

"Nothing, just your new avatar. It's fierce."

"Yeah, I'm not resting on pretty." The avatar dashed across the screen and leaped over a fence, a weapon like a paintball gun pointed toward the alley. Other non-player characters moved down the street. "Get moving."

Additional animated targets appeared on screen and Nikki quickly pushed the buttons.

Georgi said, "Watch it, you're in the way."

Nikki felt the heat on her face. "I'm moving. Hey, wait. I'm getting some kind of box flashing on my monitor."

"I don't see a box."

"Not in the game. The computer. It's about half the size of the screen."

"Start your malware."

"I can't believe anything got past the firewall." Nikki twisted the keyboard and furiously typed to open the app. "Great. Now I have a billion boxes."

"Turn off the computer."

"It doesn't look like a virus." Nikki leaned toward the screen.

"So you're an expert now? What does it look like?"

"I told you—a box. Wait. There's a message. It says: *Welcome to Camp Iris, where all the colors of the rainbow belong. Explore your truths and join your new friends in a Color War tournament.* There's a link."

"Don't hit it."

"But I'm curious."

Georgi yelled, "Just turn off the computer."

With a few clicks, the screen went black. She picked up her cell and typed to Georgi. R U coming over to fix?

A few dots flashed. You suck…

Nikki stared at the blank computer screen. With a sigh, she pulled off her headphones. She went back to her cell phone, opened Pokémon, and scrolled, looking for any new research projects. Nothing. She closed her eyes.

Ten minutes later she heard her mother greet someone at the door. Footsteps approached from the stairs. She opened her eyes.

Georgi appeared at her side. "Hey."

"Here." Nikki rebooted the computer and shoved over the keyboard.

Georgi began typing and said, "Your mom says I should stay for dinner."

"You can have my dead cow."

"Gross. And, no, I'm not watching another video about how great vegetarianism is for your body. I don't care." Georgi wiggled the mouse and then tapped the keyboard.

"Can you fix it?"

"Of course." She tapped the button on the mouse. "There."

Nikki watched the screen as the program scrolled through the files, a bar filling with blue as Georgi scrutinized each section.

"I don't think it's going to open again." Georgi faced her. "What did the box say again?"

"Just a camp Color War."

"What the heck is a Color War?"

"I have no idea." Nikki's fingers wiggled over her phone screen as she typed in a few keywords. After a few moments, she announced, "It's a thing they do at band camp, I guess."

"That's weird. You don't even play an instrument. Why would they invite you?" Georgi turned her attention back to the computer. "It's all clean. Thank goodness you shut it off in time."

"Thank goodness you can fix anything." Nikki jabbed Georgi.

Georgi poked her back. "Yes, I can. And I brought a new game."

❧ ❧ ❧ ❧

Nikki held open the screen door. "Bye, Georgi. Thanks for fixing the computer."

"No biggie. See ya."

Nikki pulled the door shut and popped up the stairs to the kitchen. A split-level meant constantly climbing stairs. She stopped and pulled open the refrigerator.

Her mom said, "Dinner is in an hour. Ed is already on his way home."

Nikki took a cheese stick and nudged the door closed. Picking at the wrapper, she peeled the string cheese with her teeth.

"Did you have fun with your game?"

"Mom, it wasn't a play date."

"I would have gotten drink boxes if it was." Her mom laughed at her joke. Then she paused for a moment, and her face got serious. "Sit down."

Nikki pulled out a stool at the counter.

"So, you and Georgi have been friends a long time."

"I guess."

"Anything more going on there? I love you no matter what. I hope you know that I'm here for you, and that you can talk to me about anything that's going on."

"Nothing is going on."

"Anything at all, anyone you're thinking about dating. Your cousin Roger is gay. His mom told me. I suppose it might just be a phase."

Nikki crammed the cheese in her mouth and stood. "Gotta go." She skipped up the stairs two at a time, went into her room, and locked the door. *Loves me no matter what, jeesh. She'll look past it if I'm queer and still love me.* Just a phase. Like when she wanted mac and cheese every day for a month? That kind of phase? Georgi was cute, and they were best buds, but not in a romantic sort of way. *What is a romantic way?* She sure wasn't like the girls that fawned over the football guys. Maybe she did like Georgi. Was that weird? Not weird, and no, she didn't like Georgi that way. Whatever that way was. And she was absolutely not talking to her mom about any of it.

❧ ❧ ❧ ❧

On her bed, Nikki caught the rubber ball and tossed it again at the wall. It thumped and bounced back toward her.

Her stepsister, Casey, yelled from the next room, "Knock it off! I can't hear my music."

Nikki leaned over and punched a button on the computer, and music blasted from the tiny speakers. She yelled, "Better?"

The door to her room flew open. "You're a jerk."

"And you're supposed to knock."

"Why? All you do is stare at a screen all day."

"What if I was changing?"

"Into what? A frog, so some princess would kiss you?"

Nikki flew from the bed and grabbed her arm. "Take that back."

"Let go of me, you freak." Casey twisted away.

Nikki's mother came to the door. "Enough. You two had better learn to get along or I'll put you in the same bedroom just to spite you both. I'm not kidding."

Casey said, "My dad wouldn't let you."

Nikki stuck out her tongue then mimicked Casey, "My dad wouldn't let you."

Mom put her hands on her hips. "Your father and I are a team. Don't press it, young lady. Both of you get equal treatment around here."

Nikki seethed. Equal wasn't what they needed. It was like becoming a twin as a teenager.

Casey turned crimson. "I'm calling my mom."

"Go right ahead. And please ask her to come here for the Fourth of July picnic. Then we're doing the concert and fireworks in the park."

Nikki crossed her arms over her chest. Another holiday ruined with all the stepmonsters. Perfect.

Casey grabbed her bedroom door but froze before slamming it.

Her mom plastered on a plastic smile. "I know you love her potato salad better than mine."

"Whatever." She shut the door.

Nikki had to admit she liked it too. She flopped onto her bed and stared at her shelves. The plastic softball trophy was losing the glue to her name tag. She should throw it out. Everyone got one. Several girls still played on the high school team. She hated playing, partly because she sucked and partly because the other girls were too serious. To be fair, she was pretty good at fielding and her arm wasn't bad. It wasn't her fault she couldn't get the hang of batting. She'd been walked a couple times but never gotten a hit. Probably because she backed out of the box. That wasn't her fault. The coach beaned her in the shoulder the first practice and she never could trust a pitch again.

She was a lot like her dad, both in appearance and interests. He wasn't much of an athlete. She missed him. When she was little, he'd read to her and yawn the whole time until he was asleep in the chair, and then she'd crawl off and go play. Maybe her gaming was like her dad's reading—introspective and solitary. She enjoyed solo activities or one-on-one interactions online rather than an organized group activity. Maybe she was even more like him than she had thought.

A steady bass beat permeated her room. Casey

practiced her cheer dance routines, stomping and clapping for hours to the same song. It was fine with her mom if she disturbed Nikki, but heaven forbid Nikki disturb Casey. It was totally unfair. Nikki picked up her ball and resumed tossing it at the wall.

Chapter Two
June 5

On Monday, Nikki dragged herself out of bed at noon. She used the bathroom and staggered to the kitchen for some juice. Her mother handed her snail mail. Her mom's face was frozen, but Nikki sensed that she knew what it was.

"You got something in the mail."

Nikki stared at the envelope sealed with wax. Who did that? Some hundred-year-old grandma? She picked open the seam and an embossed card was the only item inside. "Welcome to Camp Iris, home of the Color War tournament, a safe space for the exploration of LGBTQ identification. Please confirm your attendance."

Emily Morgan had called Nikki a lesbian and numerous derivations since elementary school. Maybe everyone else knew before she did, but ever since eighth grade, Nikki kept it to herself when she considered if she was queer. There was no reason to say it out loud until she was sure, although what would make her sure? What exactly was the criteria? A girlfriend? It might, but then again, she'd seen plenty of girls online who said they experimented with each other for fun and still called themselves straight. Not even a girlfriend would make it concrete. Besides, Nikki did not want to be an experiment. It was too bad BuzzFeed didn't have a quiz she could take. They did have a test about how lesbian you were, and that made two assumptions.

First, that the person taking the quiz already identified as queer, and second, that knowing lesbian icons meant you were a lesbian, too. That seemed suspect.

But acknowledging this card made it official. Didn't it?

Her mother cleared her throat. "So, what did you get?" Her voice was a little too high to not already know the answer.

Nikki squinted and replied, "Junk mail. I don't know how they got my address."

"Big brother. Are you sure you didn't sign up for something on your phone?" Her mother pushed up her glasses. Not an unattractive woman, she had dark hair and a round face. Her blue dangling earrings contrasted her caramel skin.

Nikki had the same light coloring as her father, although to be fair, staying in the basement all day didn't help her pallor. Her birth parents got divorced before she started kindergarten. Until last year, Nikki and her mom lived in an apartment; they moved after Mom got remarried. The house was pretty much the same as every other house in the subdivision. Winimac, New York had some cool old houses downtown, but they couldn't afford to live there. Now they had Ed and his daughter Casey. It was unfortunate that she and Nikki were in the same grade at school. More so for Nikki, since Casey was popular. Nikki tended to have just a few friends, or at least some people to have lunch with. Her best friend had been Georgi since elementary school. Georgi had an eclectic taste in clothing, hair styles, and was wicked smart.

For her part, Nikki tried to fly under the radar. She wore a lot of black and aimed for a steady B average. That was good enough to appease her mother, yet not so brainy as to draw attention to herself from either teachers or other students.

Nikki studied her mother. She was hiding something. "Mom?"

"Yes." Her mom didn't look up. Something was fishy.

"Have you ever heard of a Color War?"

"You could Google it, but I think Mrs. Black said her niece did one over the holidays last year. I think it's those races where people splash you with paint when you run by."

"Sounds horrifying."

"The race or the splash?" Her mom looked hopeful. She ran cross country in high school and kept nudging Nikki to follow in her footsteps.

Nikki shrugged. "Both. Whatever it is, count me out."

Her voice still a little too high, Mom asked, "The Color War thing. Is that a camp?"

"I guess."

Her mom cleared her throat. That wasn't a good sign. "I might have signed up to get the information."

"Why?"

"You and I don't talk much about that sort of thing."

Nikki stared at her mother. "For a very good reason."

"This camp is for young people who are questioning."

"What are you telling me?"

"Oh, come on. You must know that I know, or sort of know. You're part of the ATL, QAT, BLT, or some such thing. Whatever it is, I love you."

Nikki was speechless. She shoved the envelope in

her pocket and retreated to her room. On her iPad, she typed in the address from the envelope. The image of a corporate facility popped onto the screen. With a flick, she enlarged the writing. There were some political links, and at the very bottom, a notation about Camp Iris. Who went to camp in the city? Maybe the camp was somewhere else. She scrolled around, but there wasn't any other information. She hovered her arrow over the "Sign Up Now" button. A box popped open labeled "Need More Info?"

She tapped the glass and a video started. A man in a suit, reading from a prompter, no doubt, welcomed them to a summer extravaganza of self-exploration and validation. Rainbow ribbons twirled behind him. At the end of the message, he suggested the links for parent information and thanked them for listening. Another pop-up offered packing suggestions.

There was no way Ed would pay for it. The price must have been high, as she couldn't find it listed anywhere. Nikki anticipated two weeks of bliss when Casey went to cheer camp—alone in the basement, gaming uninterrupted all day, every day. Now that was a vacation, and it couldn't get here soon enough. She powered up her GameStation. There was no way she was going anywhere this summer. Her vacation was in the basement.

And she waited with bated breath.

Chapter Three
June 9

Nikki settled next to Georgi in the comfortable sectional couch in the cool basement. "Can I ask you something?"

Georgi sat her controller in the charging cradle. "Yeah."

"Did you get any mail recently?"

"Just the email from school on the band schedule. Why?"

"Not an email. Snail mail." Nikki handed Georgi the rainbow-colored card.

Georgi looked up, and her eyes squinted tight. She held up the invitation and studied the message. "Why would I get one too?"

Nikki paused. Her palms became damp and she rubbed them on her shorts. Why would Georgi get one, since she was presumably cis-het? Maybe she wasn't. Nikki could just ask, but shouldn't she just know? How could that be, if she didn't even know if she herself was a lesbian? "I don't know. I think it's some LGBT event. I guess it means, you know, that I'd belong there."

Georgi looked at Nikki. "Only you would know." She flipped the card over, read for a moment, and then shrugged. "Seems like fun."

Nikki avoided the queer aspect. "I was just sort of surprised. To get it, I mean. I'm not going to camp. Casey goes to camp, not me."

Georgi paused for a second. "I think you should

go. I mean, you could make friendship bracelets and crap like that."

"I'd rather play." She waved her controller.

Georgi scowled, her voice tight. "How long before you were going to tell me?"

"That I got mail?"

"No, that you like girls."

"I don't know. I don't like labels, I'm just me."

"And we've been best friends for years and you didn't trust me. Have you told anyone else?"

"I barely told myself."

"I can see that it would be easier if you got a letter or something." Georgi tilted her head, then shrugged. "You did get a letter. So now you know."

"I mean, it's kind of weird I got the card and didn't know I should. Officially." Nikki dropped her voice to a whisper. "Are you mad?"

"You do know that I knew. Or strongly suspected. We just don't talk about stuff like that."

Nikki picked at a fingernail. "Do you still like me?"

"No. We've been friends since second grade, but now that you're queer, I can't stand to be around you."

"I knew it." Nikki stiffened. Maybe Georgi was afraid she had a crush on her or something. She looked over and Georgi was grinning.

"Dang, Nikki, I'm kidding, girl. Half the band is queer or questioning. I'm pretty secure in my crush on Charles. As long as you don't start playing Muddy Heights, we're good."

"Muddy Heights? That game where you try to line up your character and poop on targets?"

The best friends fell into a fit of giggles.

Georgi jabbed Nikki. "Which makes me wonder

just how intelligent you really are."

Nikki laughed. "You're way smarter than me, but it's a fair point. That is the stupidest game."

Georgi looked thoughtful, then asked, "What if you start dating chicks smarter than me?"

"There aren't any chicks smarter than you."

Georgi nudged Nikki. "You're right."

June 10

Midmorning the next day, the doorbell chimed and Casey yelled down to the basement, "Hey, someone's at the door for you."

Nikki pressed pause and untangled herself from the blanket and the cat. Climbing the stairs, she peered through the side glass at the person on the porch. On closer inspection, she couldn't discern the gender of the tall, slender person wearing a bright yellow dress with red high heels. A mountain of blond hair coiled over their ebony skin, highlighted with bright eyeshadow and red lipstick that was perfectly applied. She didn't recognize her, but nevertheless she opened the front door and said, "Hi. Can I help you?"

"Good morning. I'm Sunshine Fanta, of the Haus of Fanta. I am Camp Iris's director." The voice was low, and at close range, Nikki could see the five o'clock shadow under the makeup. She handed her a card identical to the one she'd received in the mail.

Sunshine cleared her throat. "We haven't received your confirmation for Camp Iris, where all the colors of the rainbow belong. Home of the infamous Color War."

She opened a purse and rummaged, then pulled out a business card. "I'm sorry, but I still struggle to get it all correctly." She cleared her throat and read, "Welcome to the LGBTQQIP2SAA rainbow community. You may know that LGBTQQIP2SAA stands for lesbian, gay, bisexual, transgender, questioning, queer, intersex, pansexual, two-spirit, androgynous, and asexual."

Nikki tipped her head. "Uh…"

She tucked the card back into the purse. "Don't worry, girl. You don't need to pick a letter now, and even once you've found your lane, you can change any time you feel the need."

"Uh…"

Sunshine handed Nikki an envelope. "This contains all the information you need about the schedule. There's a packing list of what to bring, and also what not to bring. If your parents are interested, there's a contact number for PFLAG. The local group comes every year to our grand finale, the Showcase. I hope your adults would attend the program. Those theater kids are amazing."

Nikki remembered her manners. "You want to come in?"

Sunshine nodded. "If you would like to visit for a bit, I would be happy to try and answer any questions you might have."

Nikki pulled back the door. "Mom? Can you come here?"

Sunshine sashayed into the entryway. Looking around, she nodded her head and said, "I love the woodwork." She reached out a hand as her mom approached. "So nice to meet you. I'm Sunshine Fanta, of the Haus of Fanta. I'm on my way to the library to read for children's story hour, and I thought I'd stop since I was nearby. I'd like to explain the opportunities of Camp Iris to you and Nikki, if you have a moment."

Her mom blinked a few times and then said, "Would you like an iced tea?"

"I'd be delighted."

No one spoke as she filled the glasses and then set them on the table. The cuckoo clock chimed, and the dancers twirled to the music.

Sunshine Fanta went to sit down and her gown caught on the corner. With a tug, she loosened the fabric. "Not today, Satan."

Nikki slid the card toward her mom. "She's here because I haven't RSVP'd for camp and they want me to go."

Sunshine's red nails hit the glass as she picked it up, then she sipped the tea. "This is very refreshing. Thank you." She set the glass down and then folded her hands. "Camp Iris is about two hours north of here as the crow flies. Camp is an annual event for young people that are exploring the rainbow community, which is why people call it Color Camp sometimes. There is no pressure for anyone to identify anything but cis-hetero, but a great majority find the opportunity validating and informative. I've enclosed information about a small gathering for parents and adults of first-time campers. Another parent will lead the discussions, if you are interested, and it can help you explore your emotions during this journey."

Nikki gasped like the air had left the room.

Sunshine continued. "Camp lasts for four weeks. There are a variety of daily activities to select from, the usual camp-type things and a few more specialized classes geared to queer youth. There are six gender-neutral cabins, sorted by age. The number of attendees increases as they get older, although some of these kids are pretty young when they identify as queer. Each camper can also request a private room and bath, if they feel it's necessary, no questions asked. Trust me, no matter where they're assigned, somehow they all end up hanging out in one room or another anyway."

Her mother said, "Every flower blooms when it's ready. I signed up for information thinking it might be an opportunity to talk about her feelings. I mean, she's not said anything to me, but I've wondered on occasion. Her sister is also in high school and boy crazy. Always hanging out with a gaggle of friends. Nikki might meet some new friends. Maybe this camp will be good for us all...I mean, Nikki and me. I'm not sure my husband will be too thrilled."

"He won't care. It's not like I'm his kid," Nikki added.

Mom ignored the statement. "I'm not sure we can afford a second camp. Her sister—"

"Stepsister."

"Is going to cheer camp."

"We have several major corporate sponsors with very deep pockets. There is no charge, but we do accept donations at the final performance. If you have any other questions, my contact information is in the packet. Because we draw heavily from the tri-state area, we provide transportation. A bus will be at the Timber Creek High school to pick up students from this part of town." Sunshine stood. "I look forward to your acceptance email and will see you in a few weeks."

**

Saturday afternoon, the alarm on Nikki's phone chimed. Georgi's face popped on the screen. The online weekly Dungeons and Dragons game would be starting soon. It was a good quest, but Nikki was tired of her bard character. She wanted to be something more exciting in the next adventure, maybe a dwarf barbarian. Or an orc. She scrolled on the computer and found the link. Georgi's face appeared in the game room, but no one else was there yet.

Hey, can we chat? Nikki typed in a private message.

Not much time, but OK.

I think I'm going to the Iris Camp thing.

I'll miss you.

Nikki paused. Just a regular friend miss her, or something more miss her? Maybe Georgi had a crush on her all this time and she hadn't noticed. There should be directions for this sort of thing.

Same here, she wrote.

The Dungeon Master popped on, as did two other players. "Toby can't make it today. Shall we get started?"

Nikki followed along, but her thoughts kept going back to camp. Would Georgi be jealous if Nikki found new friends, or even a girlfriend? Georgi was a confident person on the outside, but they both were behind a computer screen. It was the face-to-face interactions that challenged them.

Casey passed by carrying a laundry basket. "Your mom says to put the load in the washer in the dryer when it's done. She'll fold."

Nikki didn't look up. "Fine."

"Girl chaser."

That seemed unnecessary. No one on the screen responded as if they heard Casey. What would people at school say about this whole camp thing? Mom said that she shouldn't care what her classmates thought, but that was easy to say and hard to do. Nikki barely recognized she might be a lesbian, and this was more of a declaration, even if Fanta said it wasn't. She'd bet her GameStation that there wasn't a single cis-het kid at this Camp Iris. She would look and see. Iris. Look. See. She laughed at the pun.

The voice in her ear startled her. "Faun, wouldn't you want to cast a spell to protect your teammate?"

Nikki grabbed her dice and rolled. "I got a twelve. The spell lasts ten minutes."

"And the shark bites at his leg but misses. How far can you move on one turn?"

Nikki zoned out again.

Chapter Four
June 13

Inside the large manila envelope were multiple forms including a sample of activities, medical questions, contact information for families, and a required permission form.

Please list all medications and dosages, as well as any over-the-counter drugs your child may require. To ensure their safety, we have dedicated staff members on-site who are certified in Med-Admin, ready to administer your child's medication as prescribed.

Our cabins are gender neutral. All of our campers will use private changing rooms. These rooms could be restrooms, shower stalls, or our new changing stations which are locked stalls. Counselors always supervise these areas if campers are using them. Campers do not change in public spaces, including in their cabins with other campers.

All campers have multiple bathroom options, including access to all-gender bathrooms and showers (which feature full doors that lock), as well as the boys' and girls' bathroom and shower facilities. Expectations in these spaces are reviewed at the start of camp, and they are supervised by staff.

Nikki scanned the list of suggested items to pack and wondered who these people were. Fourteen shirts? Twelve pairs of shorts? One or two swimsuits with full coverage of the chest. Six pairs of pajamas. She would have to scrounge to find more than one set.

Usually, she slept in a T-shirt if it was cold. Flat sheets or a sleeping bag? Her sleeping bag was from middle school and the Pokémon motif was probably okay for a gamer, but other teenagers would find it hilarious. She had better take sheets and a blanket. She twirled a lock of hair. This whole camp thing was a bad idea.

No laptops. That sucked. Cell phones and tablets were allowed. Maybe they had a computer lab, otherwise she'd miss her Dungeons and Dragons, although they could go old school. It seemed likely she'd find at least a few adventurers. Should she bring her dice set? Maybe not her favorite ones—the black metallic with gold markings—but just the plain sets, the blue and the red with white printed on them. Would two sets be enough? She could use the app on her phone, if it was allowed.

July 15

Through the blinds, the sunrise edged an orange glow into the room. Nikki'd been up since four a.m., afraid she'd miss her alarm. A duffel bag, a backpack, and a suitcase stood by the door. She ignored the phone in her hand, instead staring out the window mulling all the things that could go wrong. She wasn't exactly outdoorsy. She wasn't very crafty. What was she? Maybe that was the whole point.

Following a soft knock, her mom's voice came through the door. "You ready, honey?"

"Yeah," Nikki said, standing.

Her mother opened the door. "For the record, I'm glad you decided to go. Can I carry something?"

"No, thanks, I got it." Nikki put a backpack strap over each shoulder, plopped the duffel in front of the suitcase handle, and then wheeled the stack into the hallway.

They climbed the stairs without speaking, the bags banging on each step. At the front door, her mother asked, "You got everything?"

Nikki bit at her lip. "I think so."

Her mother took an envelope and tucked it into a pocket of the backpack. "Fifty bucks. My father did this for me when I went to Europe in college. This will pay for anything you forgot, so stop worrying about it."

"Thanks." Nikki smiled.

"You're welcome. You want breakfast? Never mind. I'm sure you're too wired to eat." She pushed open the front door and held it for her daughter. "Your chariot awaits."

At the SUV, Nikki put her gear in the back. She closed the hatch and startled when her stepdad appeared at her side.

Ed put his hands in his pockets. "Trying to sneak off without saying goodbye?"

Nikki gazed at him.

"Look, I know we are still trying to navigate this Brady Bunch thing, but I wanted to say. Um. Well, here." He took out his right hand and gave her several folded bills. "Please don't get any piercings or tattoos."

Nikki was sure he thought he was funny, but she also knew he wasn't kidding around about it either. She smiled. "Thanks, Ed."

He patted her shoulder and said, "See you later."

The engine started and Nikki took the hint. She got in the car, put on her seat belt, and shoved her earbuds in. The ride to the pickup spot was short, and even though they were early, a dozen people milled under the awning.

Her mom said, "You know you can text and we'll come get you if you want to come home."

"Mom, I'll be fine."

"I'll miss you. Have a good time." Her face froze into a smile.

"Bye." Nikki heard the hatch pop open. She leaned and pushed the door open, slinging her backpack on as she stood. She wrestled the bags out of the back, closed the hatch, and put up a hand. "Thanks. See you."

The distinctive rush of air brakes caused her to turn. A plain white bus pulled up, the destination sign flashing "Camp Iris." She watched as the driver came down the steps. His navy-blue slacks and light blue shirt seemed professional enough. Tufts of white hair stuck out from under his hat, and his glasses made his eyes look three times too big. With a quick step, he opened the underneath storage bin doors. Straightening up, he turned. "Good morning. If you would please, just slide your bags in the bin and you may take one item to put in the overhead." He looked at a young man with painted jeans and a tight tank top with a braided bag over his shoulder. "You may also bring any type of satchel or purse, or whatever you have that's a small bag, if you can fit it under the seat."

Nikki went toward the bus, considering which compartment to use. At a gap in the crowd, she leaned in and swung each bag into an empty spot. Holding the strap of the backpack against her chest, she stood still for a moment.

A familiar snide voice behind her said, "Nikki Po-dumb-ski. I shoulda figured you'd be here sooner or later."

Ironically, her lifelong tormentor was a lesbian

also—or at least questioning. The bile came up in her throat. Maybe she should text Mom and just go home now. These weeks would be hell with Emily Morgan anywhere near her. Ever since third grade, they circled each other like sharks, ready to shred the other. In eighth grade, they came to a sort of understanding that they should keep apart. At least, that was Nikki's understanding. Until now.

Emily was athletic and mean. She had gorgeous blond hair, typically trapped in a ponytail. Nikki stared into her sharp blue eyes. "Just keep away from me."

Emily cackled. "Not a problem."

Nikki watched her feet as she climbed the steps into the bus, careful to take a seat as far from Emily as she could. She adjusted her earbuds and watched the last campers maneuver down the bus aisle, juggling personal items. She allowed herself a glance back to see where Emily sat. The huge dude with shaggy hair seemed an odd bench mate, but they were chatting away like best friends. He wore a tank top with the imprint of a football team logo from their crosstown rivals.

He noticed Nikki, and whatever he said to Emily caused her to give an animated reply with her cheeks crimson. Emily could get as mad as she wanted—Nikki was going to camp and somehow manage to enjoy herself, just to spite Emily.

Nikki's mother often said that gaming the day away wouldn't lead to an education, let alone a career. Neither would Camp Iris, but it might lead to more gamer friends. That would be epic.

Chapter Five

Nikki adjusted the air vent over her seat and was thankful no one sat next to her. She changed her music and then watched as the city blocks flipped past. It could be in any city in America. All the same fast-food chain restaurants, the same big box stores, and the same gas stations. Even the high school looked like every other—brick with a long, covered walkway, surrounded by acres of parking. Unlike some high schools with students who drove fancy new cars, the kids at her school drove a variety of used family vehicles and some clunkers. Those that had a car were lucky; she still rode the bus. She didn't have driver's ed until the fall, even though she had turned sixteen in the spring. It wouldn't matter anyway. There was no car in her near future. Her stepfather, Ed, was a car fanatic, but no one was allowed to even breathe on his black 1979 Pontiac Trans Am with the gold firebird on the hood and matching pinstripes. He installed a CB radio just like the *Smokey and the Bandit* movies from the seventies, except no one ever drove the car more than two miles at a time.

She leaned against the window as they entered the highway, the driver picking the center lane. The rhythmic *cha-chunk* of the tires across the pavement buzzed under her feet. They passed the amusement park. The tops of roller coaster railings, brightly colored twists and turns, lured them closer. The benches and cages of the thrill rides poked above the wooden fencing. Water cascaded down the flume ride which, according to the advertising, was the tallest in the state. Her stomach clenched at just the thought of the drop. The cars and trucks they passed were so close she could have touched them if the window was open.

She was sure that she'd make a few friends, but could she meet someone more special? She wasn't interested in the boys at school and too frightened to approach a girl romantically. What brought her parents together? Her father was more of a bookworm, a professor at the community college. He preferred to hire a repair person for anything around the house as he believed he had better things to do than learn how a dishwasher worked. Maybe that was what drew her mother to Ed. He could fix anything with duct tape and a zip tie, or so it seemed. Whatever her parents saw in each other, it was how she got here, so there was that.

The bus exited the highway and stopped. She hadn't been on this two-lane road before. She wasn't even that curious where they were, probably somewhere near the hydro-dam. There were a million little coves on the big lake, a man-made monstrosity used to produce electricity. In the day, the water fell through the turbines and at night they pumped it back up. Nikki had gone on a tour with her family-to-be as a sort of getting-to-know-you event. It was pretty cool to see the humongous equipment. They had to wear a reflective vest and a helmet they called a bump cap. She was fixated on the size of everything, the trucks looking like toys in the high tunnels. Her future stepsister wanted to keep the bump cap, and secretly so did Nikki.

The light changed and the bus surged forward.

After another fifteen minutes, the engine slowed. At a towering stone archway, they turned at a dirt road. The passengers bounced as the tires rolled through the divots and washboard gravel. The woods were young, most of the trees no bigger than six inches around, but still the shade would be welcome. In the distance, a lake shimmered, several long docks poked out from the shore. A row of canoes painted in crazy patterns waited against the wall of lockers. A lifeguard tower stood at each end of the beach.

Abruptly, the brakes hissed and they stopped. Nikki turned her head and stared at the girders of the open-air performance stage. To the right was a large building—maybe it was a gym? On the left was a tall post replete with arrow signs pointing in every direction.

The driver took the mic and announced that they should leave bags underneath and that no one would be on the bus while they did camp orientation.

A voice called, "Sexual. You know…orientation."

The bus driver pulled the lever to open the door. "Watch your step."

The young man in the seat behind her said, "Gayly forward."

Nikki waited until the front seats had emptied before she stood. Following the other people, she creeped toward the large building, which turned out to be an auditorium. Tables with stacked packets arranged in plastic totes stood at the ready on the back row. Two people ushered them toward the tables. When she got closer, she saw the letters and found the line for M-N-O-P and stood at the back.

When it was her turn, she said, "Podolski. Nikki."

"P, p, p……here you are." He handed her a name

tag on a lanyard and a thick envelope. Welcome to Camp Iris."

Nikki accepted the packet and turned toward the music now playing at the front of the auditorium. She wandered about halfway down and picked a seat, the cushion soft but the fabric rough against her thighs as she sat.

A large map appeared on the screen at the front of the room. The auditorium they sat in was in the middle of the complex and marked with an X and "You Are Here" printed in red. At the far right, a lake formed one border of the camp. It appeared there was a campfire ring next to the open auditorium. These people took their performance space seriously. A series of buildings clustered around an outdoor pool. At the top of the map, a ring of smaller buildings formed an arch. To the far left, two open fields were bordered by a wooded area. At the bottom, the slogan "Just Be You" slow-scrolled across the full width in fancy letters.

⁂

A man in a dark blue suit with a paisley shirt and striped tie approached the podium. Some of the other campers clapped and cheered. Nikki didn't recognize him until he spoke. The smooth baritone was unmistakable, even though he wasn't dressed as Sunshine Shasta. No, it was Fanta. Whatever.

He tapped the microphone. "Good afternoon, everyone. Take a breath if you can hear me."

In moments, the auditorium fell silent. Nikki smiled. It was a brilliant technique.

"I am Mr. Novak, director. Welcome to Camp Iris, home of the Color War tournament, a safe space for the exploration of LGBTQ identification. Our first order of the day is to get you settled into your cabins so you can unpack, but I'd like to share a little history. As you may know, in Greek mythology, Iris was the personification of the rainbow, a messenger of the gods, and so naturally a rainbow goddess is the inspiration for the name of our camp. Interestingly, she was said to carry water from the river Styx, which she used to put people to sleep who perjured themselves. So here, no tea, no shade, no pink lemonade. We speak our truth, whatever that might be.

"I'm sure you're all starving, so let's get a few details worked out so we can get to dinner. And never fear, we have vegetarian, vegan, and keto choices. For your comfort, our housing consists of six gender-neutral cabins sorted by age group, plus a building with dorm rooms for free spirits. Each has a counselor that can offer you help in matters like selecting programs to participate in, how to work a clothes washer, and dealing with homesickness. Please ask any staff person if there is something we can assist with during our time together.

"Let me hear our seniors, age sixteen to seventeen."

Cheers erupted around her.

"Thank you. There are three cabins for seniors, Bearadise Den, Spruced Up Shack, and of course, Seas the Day."

Nikki thumbed through her packet. She was assigned to Seas the Day. No doubt full of nautical references. Maybe the lake was bigger than she thought, which was terrifying. She didn't mind swimming in pools with nice clear water and no monsters of any sort. She liked to see her toes and be confident that nothing was about to separate them from her body.

"Where are our juniors, ages fourteen to fifteen?"

A smattering of claps echoed around the room.

"Shy bunch. There are two cabins this year for juniors, Bluebird Bunker and Tiger Cove."

"That leaves our freshmen. How about everyone give them some help."

The thunderous applause exceeded even the initial cheers.

"Thank you. Our frosh will be in the Firefly Fortress. I ask all of our returning campers of any age to remember what it was like to be new and to include campers who might be a bit circumspect."

He raised his hands. "Every summer I predict the best camp season, and this year will far outshine the past events." Voices murmured around the room. "I know you doubt me, because last year was fabulous. But trust me." He snapped and a cascade of confetti fell from the heights of the stage, music thumped from speakers, and laser lights flicked wildly around the room.

The audience leaped up and joined his dance, the crowd undulating as one. The music drifted away, and he approached the microphone again. "Please double-check your initial housing assignment, and if you disagree, tell your counselor on arrival and they will transfer you accordingly. Thank you for joining us. You won't be disappointed."

The house lights came up, and Nikki tugged her backpack to her shoulder. Following her row out of the auditorium, she glanced around for the signs to each cabin.

A fishnet filled with shells and paper aquatic animals hung over the porch entry. A sign declared this "Seas the Day" in blue letters on white. Inside, the scent of sweaty teenagers with a dash of mold and bleach betrayed the location as a camp cabin. A young woman with a cap over her red hair topped with wire rim sunglasses held a clipboard and marked it as she spoke with each approaching camper.

Nikki waited her turn. "Nikki."

"Right. Hacker or gamer?"

Nikki's eyes widened.

"Just kidding. I'm Miranda, she/her, and I'm also in charge of the Yellow Team for the Color War, and I saw your name on the list. Anything gadget related belongs with us. Be prepared to have to fix stuff once people find out you're an Owl. Of course, cabins are mixed, so we won't discuss any team secrets here. There's a schedule for cabin chores that have to be done before breakfast, which starts at eight. The counselors get judged, and we get points on how clean things are. I'm used to winning a lot of points. Anyway, welcome, and go pick a bunk." Miranda handed her a slip of paper. "That's our cabin Wi-Fi and password. I upgraded the modem. There's a camp Wi-Fi, but it's usually pretty slow."

Nikki shoved the paper in her pocket and walked into the room, guessing it held eight to ten bunks.

A guy wearing jean shorts, a black tank top, and a rainbow cape approached. "I am Daniel, he/him. Welcome to the Haus of Daniel."

A young woman leaned out from under a bunk. "It is not. I'm McKenzie. She/her." She reached out a hand that Nikki shook. "That's Jesse cranking out the tunes—they/them. We're all on Team Yellow. The other dudes there are probably in the orange group. Political. Sheila on that top bunk, Quinn on the bottom."

Over their cubicles, each already had hung posters with assorted slogans relating to global warming and trans rights.

A guy with a mountain of curly hair stood. He pushed up his black-framed glasses over his chestnut-brown eyes. "Greetings and salutations. I'm Hunter, they/them." He pulled back an imaginary bow and arrow. "Elf king and friend to all."

McKenzie said, "I think there's still a couple bunks by the windows."

Nikki adjusted her backpack and went toward the back. She spotted a camper bent over making her bed. Nikki froze in her tracks. On one side of her head, she had her long hair woven into a braid. The other side was shaved, and a bandanna wrapped her crown. Her clothes were unremarkable, just a tank top over shorts, but it was those long legs that captivated Nikki.

She noticed the attention and smiled. "Hi. I'm Caitlyn." She pointed to her name on the bunk. Caitlyn Baudelaire. "It's pronounced Boh-deh-lair, but everyone calls me Gumball. She/her. Welcome to the best cabin, or at least the smartest. This your first year? This is my third. Early bloomer, I guess."

"Nikki. Um, she/her. Yeah, first year." She scanned the room. It seemed most beds were already loaded with personal items as people unpacked. The best thing was that there was no Emily Morgan. There was hope Camp Iris wouldn't suck after all.

"Top's open here, if you don't mind climbing. I promise I don't snore."

Nikki had hoped for a bottom bunk. "Thanks."

Now how was she supposed to get up there? She stepped onto the end of the rack, grabbed a nearby rafter, and swung up onto the mattress.

"Are you sure you don't belong with the athletes? That was pretty smooth."

"Definitely not. Just wait until I try to get down."

Gumball grinned, her eyes sparkling blue. Nikki's mouth went dry and her hands began to sweat. She returned the grin and then lay back. "I guess this will do." With a twist, she hung both feet down and then dropped to the floor.

"A gamer in goth clothing. I'm going to work on a nickname, but I'm leaning toward Airborne."

A voice from the front called out, "Hey. As you know, I'm Miranda, cabin counselor. I'm here to help you have the best four weeks possible. Maybe the best four weeks of your life, hard to say. I have a couple of announcements."

The intimate moment was gone, and Nikki listened as her mind whirled about the turn of events. She'd only been at camp an hour and already had a crush. Gumball, what a stupid nickname. It didn't matter. She probably already had a girlfriend at her school or something. Seas the Day, indeed.

Chapter Six
July 16

In the morning, promptly at seven a.m., the phone alarms started to ring. They had forty-five minutes to get ready and fifteen minutes for chores. After her shower, Nikki swept the porch as indicated on the chore chart, a large wheel listing each task that was evidently rotated each day.

Breakfast was at eight and featured a cold cereal bar, assorted bagels and toast, and a buffet with eggs, potatoes, bacon, and hot cereal. A juice bar also included milk or soda. Thank the gods. Nikki took a large glass and filled it with Coke. It was unfortunate for the older students and counselors that coffee was not presented as an option.

After the short walk from the cafeteria to the auditorium, Nikki and her cabin mates took seats together. A phone app was listed on the overhead screen. Most of the campers hastily downloaded the program.

Mr. Novak, in a crisp shirt with dress slacks, stood at the front by the podium. "Greetings, campers. It's a glorious morning at Camp Iris, and I'm sure you can't wait to get started. Today is split into two units. This morning your teams will get the first chance to brainstorm for the Showcase finale at the end of camp. This afternoon will be our program on queer history featuring a guest lecture given by a professor from the university."

Several of the counselors appeared on the edge of the stage.

"The teams all have a mascot, but most of us refer to them by color. You have been grouped with other campers with similar interests. If you feel that there may be a group you'd rather join, we can make a onetime change. After today, all teams are locked. In no particular order, first is the Cheetahs and Justin will try to keep our athletes and dancers from running all over the place. This will be the Red Team."

A tall guy with a crew cut lifted his hand and then flexed.

"Stop. You'll get them all distracted and there's no telling what chaos might follow." Mr. Novak laughed. "Okay, next is the Dolphins for our visual artists and actors, which will be green this year. Say hello, Sam."

A lanky person with long brown hair waved. Nikki wasn't sure if Sam was short for Samantha. That was the point of this camp, though, wasn't it?

"Our computer/robotics people are the Owls. Miranda will be returning for her second year as counselor. This will be the Yellow Team."

Nikki and her other Yellow Team teammates screamed and clapped.

"Goldfinch is for the musicians, both instrumental and vocal, as well as musical theater. These campers will be blue this year."

"Thomas will try to conduct this flock into order." No one laughed at his puns. "Tough audience." Everyone snickered. "Thank you. My delicate ego is soothed. Next is the political Porcupines. You're either with them or against them." He held up a fist. "Power to the people, this group will be orange again this year."

A stocky man with a slight beard walked onto the

stage with his arms in the air. He chanted, "Two, four, six, eight, who do we appreciate? Sunshine, Sunshine, Sunshine."

"Thank you, Marcus." A list flipped up on the screen. "These are the assorted classes and activities that will be offered this camp session. The full schedule and a daily schedule with class descriptions will be available in the app." A giant schedule popped onto the overhead.

"For those who are new to us, each team is awarded points during camp. The first two weeks include daily opportunities to try new skills and work with your team to create an extravaganza for the camp finale. At the official start of the Color War, your team may also be awarded random points for cooperation, enthusiasm, and fabulousness." He paused. "This is not RuPaul's drag show. There is no library here, so if there is too much reading, points will be taken away."

A voice yelled, "Give the girls what they want."

He snapped his fingers. "The fun is in the fight, so to speak, but if you are the competitive type, I might suggest that you try some new activities because you never know what might become a team competition event."

A voice behind her whispered, "We better split the list so we can cover as much as possible."

Nikki scanned the typical camp stuff on her phone app, and then wondered how they sorted the teams. Of course, by color. That was the whole Color War thing. A message popped up on her screen confirming that she was on the Yellow Team.

❧❧❧❧

Outside the auditorium, she spotted a yellow sign with an owl image surrounded by FORTRAN. She turned and went that direction. At the meeting room, another sign confirmed this was the Yellow Team. She peeked inside.

Miranda said, "Welcome. Everyone, take a laptop and sign your name and the number on this sheet. It's for your use at camp."

A large whiteboard had a website and password with directions to join by 1:30. This was way better than some icebreaker game to remember names.

Nikki and her cabin mates sat at a long table with several younger campers who were now part of Team Yellow. They were instructed to select traits for an avatar for a virtual paintball game.

Miranda said, "At the end, we'll try to figure out who was who. Except for me." A red-haired barbarian woman appeared on the screen at the same time the gamer name MagicSchoolBusDropout. "Y'all try to keep up. I ain't playing to lose."

Nikki typed in GoogleWasMyIdea and scrambled quickly to select the traits for her avatar, accidentally putting her character in pirate boots and shorts with a vest. Each avatar popped on screen holding a gun. She pushed her controller and a fluorescent orange paint ball shot out and splatted at the feet of Miranda's avatar.

Miranda's character turned and blasted Nikki. "How about you wait until we start?"

"Sorry," Nikki mumbled.

"No worries. I get a little competitive," Miranda said. "Listen up. We had one player go down already. You have three lives, not nine like a cat. Be careful."

"Guess we know who watched the most Blue's

Clues." Gumball leaned with her controller. "Let's do this."

Aaron cheered. "I almost got two at once!"

"Good one. Dang. Dang. Gotcha!" Hunter said.

"You know, the crosshairs are for aiming." Daniel laughed, then groaned. "Good one. I'm out."

Asa yelled, "Frog guts. I'm out, too."

"I've seen carousels turn faster than you." Gumball pushed the buttons frantically. "Got ya!"

McKenzie yelled, "Crap on a cracker. I'm out."

"Yes, got another one! Oh no, not the red screen of death. I'm done. Who's still in?" Hunter asked.

Nikki turned her character, blasting in a circle. "Get on the bus, we're going to school."

"Good one, Boots." Daniel stood up. "Dang it."

Miranda said, "The green-haired one has the map skills of Christopher Colombus."

Nikki ran her character behind a wall. As she blasted and ducked through the maze, she tried to figure out which avatar was Gumball. Her screen flashed red.

Miranda's character lifted both arms in victory. The real Miranda said, "I'm going to freeze the screen so we can all guess who is which avatar."

"Who was URMyPrey?"

Gumball raised her hand. "Guilty."

"And BlackStabbath?"

Daniel ran a hand through his hair. "Me."

"PewPewYaDead?"

Hunter nodded. Aaron snickered. Hunter glared at him and asked, "And you are?"

"EatBullets."

Miranda asked, "GoogleWasMyIdea?"

Nikka smiled and raised a hand.

"Good one. BadKarma?"

Elliot stood up.

"CerealKiller?"

Asa, the youngest camper, giggled. "Get it?"

Miranda smiled at him. "Yeah, we got it, Padawan. And I'm guessing McKenzie is KungFuBarbie."

McKenzie waved a hand across her body. "Pretty on the outside, killer on the inside."

"And the runner up was ProbablyCheating," Miranda said.

"Probably," Jesse said. "But with good music."

"I'm going to start calling you DJ." Gumball gave them a thumbs-up.

Miranda glanced at her phone. "Let's take a short break and meet up in ten minutes to talk about our project."

In the hall, Gumball nudged Nikki. "New nickname, Boots. But overall, the avatar suits you."

Nikki smiled, but butterflies fluttered in her chest.

❧ ❧ ❧ ❧

After the gaming icebreaker, Miranda slid back a room divider and the space expanded. They entered the half that might be a regular classroom, except it had couches and stuffed chairs in addition to tables and chairs.

Miranda stood at the front of the room. "This will be our lab for the build. No one is allowed in here except the Yellow Team. I hope you're ready to work hard together. Every year the musical theater folks crush it at the grand finale. This year, the Owls, a.k.a. Team Yellow, must dominate the camp show."

Aaron made hooting noises and everyone laughed.

"I like the enthusiasm, however, I'm not kidding. Every year the musical kids whip up some amazing skit and we look like dorks with no creativity."

Daniel shrugged. "We don't have time to program a game with Sunshine Fanta racing to find high heel shoes."

Miranda grinned. "No, but that is hilarious. We should circle around to that."

Nikki said, "We need to make robots."

Gumball stood up and walked to the front. "Excellent." She popped the cap off the dry erase marker, wrote the title of "Robotics Grand Finale," and then drew columns on the whiteboard. "Okay, people. First row is for any wild idea you get, second row is parts we might need, and the third is miscellaneous ideas that relate to the project but don't have to do with the build."

Nikki crossed her legs and leaned back. "No limitations on components?"

"Right. Other than safety, no rules, just budget." Gumball hovered the marker over the board. "How do you want these things to move?"

Daniel twirled his curly black hair, his nails painted a dark shade of blue. He said, "Flying would be awesome."

Gumball said, "Drones, excellent, but super expensive. Next."

"Well, the stage is flat, I assume. It's either wheels or legs," McKenzie said.

Nikki watched her closely. Her blond hair was pulled into a ponytail. She had cut off the sleeves of a flannel shirt, matched with cutoff jeans. Nikki found her distracting—not because she was attracted to her, but because she liked the look for herself. Maybe she needed to get a flannel shirt, if they came in black. They probably did.

Hunter, with their black-framed glasses, reminded Nikki of Clark Kent. They said, "Humanoid, or maybe like an insect?"

"Or dinosaurs! They could roar and stuff," Asa said, showing his age.

Gumball said, "Audio element. I like it. Now expand. What are they going to do?"

The silence stretched out. Finally, Aaron said, "What if we copy another team? Dance, or maybe cheers, a skit?"

McKenzie nodded. "But with robots. Killer."

"What do we need for the build?" People shouted out supplies and Gumball scribbled parts on the board. She paused.

McKenzie asked, "How big are these things? Like a foot? How is the audience going to see them?"

Gumball nodded. "It's a good point. Let's consider that a major issue." She snapped the lid on the marker and sat down.

Hunter clapped. "A video projection, except onto all their phones and iPads."

Miranda folded her legs under her in the chair. "I like it. It does assume everyone has them at the Showcase."

"And it might take our whole five minutes trying to help the audience log in," Nikki said.

"Good point," Hunter added. "What about old school and just use screens around the room?"

Gumball scribbled on the board. "Excellent suggestion. Who do we know in AV that can hook us up?"

Miranda said, "I'm guessing they already will have cameras that broadcast around the theater…like at concerts and sporting events and all. We just need to confirm."

"And then add a drone feed!" Daniel shouted.

Gumball nodded. "Yes. I like how you think. Alright, let's circle around to budget again. I can probably get my uncle to bring us some stuff."

Elliot, his eyes twinkling with excitement, said, "Who's going to program the things, and who's going to operate them? I'm pretty good with my drone at home."

"I bet everyone is good with a controller. We may have to take turns." Miranda began typing notes into her laptop. "Gumball should program. Each robot should follow the program once it's started. Let's all think about what we want them to do and then let that drive form and function."

Jesse rubbed their ear and spoke for the first time. "Maybe something like synchronized swimming."

McKenzie said, "They could line dance."

Miranda waved her hands. "Blended. Like a cheer dance troop. Big music, lights, the whole thing."

Gumball went to the board and scribbled "GO BIG." "Remember, this is about the points chase. There isn't any one element per se, it's about covering all the categories. Artistic expression, group participation, overall creativity, audience response. Our presentation must include all team members. I think we need a log book of who does what as we build so we can document our paths to success—or failure—and adjust."

Nikki nodded. "I can do that. We can all pretend to run a controller, even if only one turns on the program and it all runs automatically."

Daniel said, "I doubt the judges will understand anything about programming or robots."

The group laughed.

Gumball held up a hand. "We don't need to finalize anything today. Bring back any ideas you get to our next meeting."

"Right," Miranda said. "Let's table our concepts until our next time, then vote. Who's the biggest music nerd?"

They all pointed to Jesse.

Gumball grinned. "I guess you're the DJ. We can let the music influence design."

❧ ❧ ❧ ❧

After dinner, Nikki lay on her bunk and scrolled through online videos looking for inspiration. Imitation was the biggest form of flattery, or so her mom said, but Nikki wanted something amazing. Maybe drone lights as the backdrop, and robots on the floor. She tapped the note in her phone and kept scrolling.

Gumball popped up next to her and touched Nikki's face, the heat of Gumball's skin hot and sweaty. Nikki chose to ignore the tingle and goose bumps.

"Hey, Gumball."

"Hey." Gumball snapped the contraband gum. "You know, Nikki, I could trim up your hair a bit. I brought my clippers. I do my own hair all the time." The gum popped as she blew a bubble.

Nikki didn't doubt the close-shaved hair caused strangers to wonder her gender, but certainly the round curves of her body drew the attention of young men and women alike. Gumball was smoking hot and super cool.

"My ears stick out," Nikki said.

"No, they don't."

Nikki hated her ears. They were normal sized but stuck out, at least more than anyone in her family. Gumball didn't seem to care about her ears, which did actually stick out. Absently, Nikki touched her earlobe. "You don't think so?"

"Nope. Let's do it now." She held up an image on her tablet. "Like this sort of thing? I don't see you jumping all the way to a closer cut, not right off."

Nikki couldn't see the picture for the glare but agreed anyway. She would never consider herself one of the popular kids, but no one here knew that. It's only hair, and it would grow back. "If you think you can, sure."

"No problem. I clip our poodle, and his hair is curly. Yours will be a cinch."

Before Nikki could change her mind, a slightly damp beach towel was draped around her shoulders as she sat on the stool. At camp only two days and she erased any doubts that she was a lesbian. She felt heat on her neck as the gorgeous woman stood behind her. The warmth of Gumball's chest against Nikki's back made Nikki want to lean into her. She had been afraid to Google lesbian porn for fear someone would see her browser history. Snuggling seemed a good place to start, even if she hadn't the slightest clue what else to do. It must be a natural progression. She jumped when Gumball's fingers stroked her head.

"This has to go." She ran her hand through Nikki's hair.

"My ears stick out."

Gumball pushed back the hair. "I already told

you, they don't. Besides, how else would ears work if they were just plastered against your head? Might as well just have the ear canal and look like a dolphin or something."

Chills ran up Nikki's arm and the scent of a musky cologne teased her sinuses. As her body responded to the closeness, Nikki tried not to close her eyes. She loved having someone play with her hair and at that moment, Gumball could shave her head and she wouldn't care. "I trust you."

With a click, the clippers buzzed to life. Nikki grit her teeth as the plastic guide touched her temple. In moments the hair on almost half her head had dropped onto the floor. She wasn't convinced Gumball was wrong about her ears, but it was too late now.

"Close your eyes," Gumball instructed.

Nikki obliged. The noise of the clippers shifting around her indicated that Gumball was removing a lot of hair. The arm brushing against her shoulder stilled, and then the buzzing stopped. A soft cloth wiped her face.

"Open your eyes."

Nikki stared into the mirror, speechless. She rubbed her hand across the crew cut.

Gumball frowned. "You hate it."

"No, I don't. I just can't believe that it's me."

"It's you, Nikki. And you look rocking hot. I hope you're ready for the attention."

Nikki rubbed at her neck. "Good or bad?"

Gumball tugged the towel back. "Depends on what you want, but I'd guess you'll have your pick."

The heat rose to her cheeks and an odd butterfly sensation started in her belly.

Gumball lightly touched Nikki's cheek. "You are

adorable. You're lucky I have a girlfriend, or I might not be able to keep my hands off you."

Nikki pressed her lips together. Of course she had a girlfriend. Could she really find one herself? If that was what she wanted. Although at the moment, it was crystal clear that she was a lesbian. The word rolled in her head and, like the new haircut, it provided a whole different image of herself. Not better or worse, just different. The hair on the top of her head spiked up, fading to the sides. She stroked the short hairs over her ear. "Thanks, this looks cool."

"As cool as your avatar."

Chapter Seven
July 17

At the morning camp meeting, Thomas was at the podium in khaki shorts and a Camp Iris T-shirt under a loose flannel shirt. In what he must have mistakenly thought was a decent Canadian accent, he said, "Good day, eh?"

The crowd politely clapped.

He went back to his normal soft drawl. "Today there are several classes and the first identity-based peer groups. Please check the schedule in the app for time and location. This afternoon will be the first day for the Butterfly Closet with clothing and accessories to explore gender identities. Stop in any time between nine and four in the afternoon. You're welcome to wear out any items you care to borrow as long as you return them by the end of the day."

He pointed to his chest with the logo. "Camp items are available in the store, along with any personal items you may have forgotten. Some of you little dudes need some deodorant."

Mr. Novak cleared his throat from behind the stage.

Thomas said, "Well, they do. And in closing, just a reminder. If you want to participate in the swimming programs and water sports, you need to pass the swim test with a lifeguard prior to the event. Testing blocks are every morning at six and ten. Your swim pass will remain on the bulletin board by the lake. You do not need a pass for the pool as it's only four feet deep. Have a gay day."

As they left the auditorium, the speaker in the corner cracked and then a low voice said, "The crafting class More Than Glitter Meets the Eye will start in fifteen minutes with a change to the conference room from C to D. Also, whoever hung the boxer shorts on the direction post is requested to cease and desist. Thank you."

Gumball nudged Nikki. "Boxer shorts. A prank a ten-year-old would do. Let me tell you something."

They stepped off the sidewalk and sat on a bench.

Gumball took out a package of gum and offered a stick to Nikki. "There's this little rivalry between the jocks and the gamers. The Red Team tries to do all these pranks, but this year they are going down in flames."

"Pranks aren't allowed."

"Getting caught isn't allowed. Besides, there's always someone else trying something and it throws the staff off our scent. This year, Emily is going down."

"Wait. Emily Morgan, by chance?"

Gumball nodded. "You know her?"

"You could say that. We go to Timber Creek."

"Good. Maybe you'll have insider information. Anyway, we've both been here for three years. The first year we stayed in the same cabin and started a tradition. Last year we tried to outdo each other. And now, this summer, I have a new assistant."

"Who?"

"You."

Nikki pursed her lips. As much as she didn't want to get in trouble, this would be an opportunity to spend time with Gumball alone. Presumably. "How many people do you work with?"

"I have a couple of outliers I toss ideas to, but it's just you and me for the best stuff. Hey, I gotta go. I'll see you later." With that, Gumball was gone.

Nikki decided now was as good a time as any to take the swimming test. Plus, she'd have extra days if she didn't pass the first time and needed to retake the test. She went to the cabin and changed clothes. As she stepped out on the porch, she stopped to admire the lake in the distance, smooth as glass. Nikki made her way toward the center of campus and snickered when she passed the signs, now covered with assorted bras. Maybe it was Gumball. Maybe it wasn't. Either way, it was funny.

At the beach, she paused to steady her nerves. She tugged at her top. She had barely passed swimming class at school and that was in a nice, safe, chlorine pool. Lakes were full of things that could nibble or stab, or even yank you under. The water here was murky, where surely monster fish hung out waiting to bite the toes of unsuspecting campers. She shuddered.

A lifeguard in a white tank top and red trunks picked up a bullhorn. Nikki was glad they had a policy of a top when swimming so the campers exploring gender lines would feel more comfortable.

He said, "Print your name on the clipboard for your badge. Line up on the dock. There's no reason to go one at a time. You have to dive in, swim across to the rope on the other side, and then back using any stroke you want."

Nikki took the clipboard and wrote her name. She handed it to a young camper beside her. A group of people approached. At first glance, it could be the swim team for the Olympics, all of them muscular, some wearing body suits, even rubber caps and goggles. In the middle of this display of athleticism was Emily Morgan. Of course.

Emily said, "If the lifeguard can't get you fast enough, I bet one of us can drag you out."

Nikki squinted her eyes. "I wouldn't let you touch me even if I was drowning."

"Have it your way." She took the towel from around her neck and started to stretch her arms, the tanned skin flexing.

Nikki was transfixed. The blue swimsuit left nothing to the imagination, and for an athlete she was pretty chesty. Bending to reach a foot, Nikki almost fainted when the suit crept up into her butt cheeks, evidently made of steel.

The sound of a whistle interrupted her survey of the woman. She laid her towel on the bench, carefully set her sunglasses on top, and stood near the edge of the dock, her teeth chattering either from nerves or the cool air, or both.

The lifeguard climbed into the seat on the ladder. "Anytime you're ready. It's not a race."

The hell it wasn't. Nikki was a good diver, and she broke the surface first, bodies splashing in around her on both sides. The cold caused her to gasp, but she quickly settled into her rhythm for the front crawl. Three strokes, breath, three strokes, breath on the other side. Repeat. Repeat. Any snakes or turtles would be long gone from the commotion. The water churned near her as other swimmers passed. The water seemed deep. Could she stand up if she needed to? Panic gripped her chest and she struggled to breathe. She switched to gasp a breath every other stroke. Maybe she couldn't retake the test? She had assumed that she might be able to. If she should flunk, she'd miss out on all the swim parties, or worse, she'd have to attend wearing a life jacket.

She reached out for the floating blue rope, yellow buoys with bells holding it in position. She touched and simply turned. A fancy flip was out of her range of skills, and she was as likely to end up on the other side of the boundary as inside the rope. She was still in the middle of the swimmers, some paddling toward her. With a deep breath she started forward again, wondering if she would look like a wimp if she switched to the backstroke to breathe easier. No, then she might swim right into the dock. She forced her burning thighs to kick more furiously.

Emily was just in front of her. Concentrating on form, she willed her body to go faster. Just as she touched the dock, she sensed a body nearby and then her head slammed forward. The clunk echoed under the planks. She flailed, and a set of hands grabbed hers and tugged her upward. Another set of hands pulled her completely out of the water. The metallic taste of blood from her lip infuriated her. She forced her feet down to stand, but instead found herself dizzy.

"I'm Cameron. You'll be fine. Just have a seat. I'll get some help." The lifeguard put an arm around her and guided her toward a beach chair.

How the hell did she run into the dock? Someone must have pushed her.

Emily walked past, seemingly unconcerned about Nikki.

Nikki glared and resisted the urge to flip her off. That little bitch pushed me, and now I look pathetic.

The lifeguard handed her a small towel. "Hold this ice on your mouth. I think you need it for your forehead, too. Next time, maybe slow down, Ledecky."

"Ledecky?"

"The Olympic swim champion."

"Ah, right." Nikki looked around. *Didn't anyone see her push me? Evidently not.*

After the last swimmer climbed out, the lifeguard picked up the bullhorn. "You all pass. I'll have your badges made up for open swimming. They'll be on the left bulletin board. You move it to the right when you get in the water and then move it back when you get out. No solo swimming. You must swim with a buddy. Thank you."

The gaggle of athletes all turned and looked at Nikki, sitting on the deck holding the towel to her mouth. It didn't matter what they said, she could tell they were laughing at her. She didn't know how, but she'd get back at them. Maybe she'd freeze all their Venmo accounts.

The lifeguard squatted to eye level. "Do you think you can walk to the first aid center?"

"Of course." She stood, then reached for his arm for balance. "Just got up too fast."

"Hmm. Well, there's a fee if you get blood on my towel." He grinned as he wrapped it around her.

Her wet skin dried on the way, but her suit was still damp and stuck to her body. Goose bumps popped up as they stepped into the air-conditioned building. At the counter, there was a sign-in sheet, so she took the pen and scribbled her name.

The lifeguard waited. A person in scrubs approached, her blond hair pulled into a ponytail. Her gray eyes were serious. "Hey, Cam. You brought my first patient of camp. Didn't take long. What happened?"

"She got tangled with another swimmer and conked her head. I just want to make sure she's okay."

"Thanks, I got it from here. Hey…" She looked at the paper. "Nikki. I'm Stephanie. Let's take a look at that lip. That lump on your forehead looks bad, but actually it's not. Sticking out is scary but mostly harmless, and I'll bet it bruises pretty by tomorrow."

"Great," Nikki mumbled.

Stephanie used a small flashlight and studied her mouth. "Dizzy?"

"Not anymore."

"Headache?"

"Yeah."

She typed into a computer. After several moments, she asked, "Last name?"

"Podolski."

"There you are. Looks like your parents authorized OTC as needed." Stephanie opened a cabinet, selected a bottle, popped the lid and shook several tablets into a paper cup. "The good news is I don't think your lip needs any stitches. Mouths heal really quick. Put ice on both your lip and forehead to help with swelling and pain. The headache should be gone by tomorrow, but the lump might take up to a week."

"Thanks." Nikki accepted the paper cup of water, took the pills, and flicked the trash toward the can. Gingerly, she shifted off the table. Camp was off to a swell start. A knot on her head should really help her attract a girlfriend.

❧❧❧❧

Nikki stretched out on the bunk, a cool washcloth over her eyes. Other than the wicked headache, she was fine physically. The entire thing was embarrassing, and she wasn't sure how to take the high road and exact retribution. Did she want people to know it was her that nailed it to Emily, or just the payback?

Gumball's voice was near. "I just heard what happened." A warm hand touched her arm. "Are you okay?"

Nikki lifted the washcloth off her face. "Just a bit of a headache. Misjudged the dock."

Gumball whispered, "I heard the whole story from Miranda, who's friends with the student director of first aid. You're lucky you didn't drown."

Nikki appreciated the loyalty, but now she knew all of camp would know what had happened. "Between you and me, I think I was pushed. I hate Emily."

"That doesn't sound right. I mean, she always seemed easygoing. Nevertheless, I already had her in my crosshairs as part of the Red Team. Let's plan the payback, or as I call it, the prankback." Gumball slid up onto the bunk next to her.

Nikki froze. Was this allowed? It was broad daylight, they were both fully dressed, and as far as she knew, Gumball wasn't interested. To be honest, Nikki was very interested. The heat from Gumball's leg against hers stirred desires Nikki wasn't sure how to express. There must be rules for dating. Or whatever. She regretted not reading her stepsister's teen magazines at least a time or two. They always had stories about how to flirt. The stagnant air did little to cool the sweat now forming on her face. Now what had Gumball been saying? It must be the bump on the head. "Sorry, say again?"

Gumball gently touched near the lump on her head. "You sure got clocked. I said that Emily is lucky

I wasn't there."

Nikki didn't doubt the intention, but Gumball would have been crushed by that crew. "We should stay in our lane."

"Exactly. I have been known to create a social media buzz a time or two."

"I don't want my pathetic accident becoming public knowledge."

"It's probably too late, but the pics on Snapchat are gone already. I was thinking more of a character assault, maybe some trolling."

Nikki put the cloth on her head. "I love your enthusiasm, but can we touch base in a while? My head is pounding."

Gumball kissed her cheek and then slid off the bed. "I hope you feel better soon. I'll go get you a slushy. That should help."

And with that, Gumball skipped down the row of bunks and out the door. Nikki peeked from under the fabric to find she was alone. Tears of frustration threatened to fall. But why? The whole incident? Emily was always an ass. The pain? Yes, that was it. And maybe the fact she got a kiss, and it was nothing to Gumball and everything to her. She found no answers before she drifted to sleep.

Nikki woke when Miranda nudged her arm. "I brought you a to-go bag from the cafeteria. I think it's a sandwich with chips and some grapes. I hope you don't have an aversion to PB and J."

Nikki sat up. "No, thanks for bringing it. I guess I slept through dinner."

"Yep. Everyone should be back in a few minutes for cabin activity time."

Nikki slid down from the bunk. She went to the

bathroom and studied her face, her lip still swollen and red, her forehead now shifting to blue and purple. She washed up and then took a seat on the porch to eat. She picked bits of sandwich and maneuvered them in her mouth without jarring her lip. She was thankful Miranda thought to bring it to her. The chips were too salty to try and the grapes too big.

Gumball skipped up the path. "Hi. Glad to see you up. I brought you an ice pop."

Nikki accepted the cold plastic strip of colored ice water. "Thanks." She tore the edge and squeezed the bottom to push the ice upward. Gently applying it to her lip, she sighed.

Hunter took a seat next to her, their long legs stretched over the steps. "You okay?"

Nikki nodded. "I feel better after my nap."

"I totally could take a nap every day." They eyed her food. "Are you going to eat that?"

She handed Hunter the chips and baggie of grapes.

"Thanks. My mom calls me the garbage disposal because I eat everything that's left over." They tore open the bag and picked out a chip. "You play D and D?"

"Of course."

"Cool. We should be able to play, both old school and online."

"I brought dice."

"Me, too. Three sets."

Miranda called out the door, "Come on in, everyone, let's get started."

Nikki followed Hunter inside.

Miranda stood in the center of the room. "Sometimes we will have evening activities for the whole camp, like a dance or bonfire, and sometimes you'll have free time. Today, we're having a cabin activity."

Gumball said, "Seas the Day."

"Exactly. I have two things planned for this evening. First, everyone can decorate their name tags. On the front table I put out some markers, sticker sheets, and some assorted jewels. Camp Iris has a new thing this year. The staff is supposed to award beads, so there's some plastic strings to tie on the lanyard. Everyone gets a blue water bead for our cabin."

Nikki considered the options while she tied on the string, careful to feed the bead through before tying the knot.

Gumball did the same and whispered, "This might be the only bead I get all camp."

Nikki snickered.

Miranda asked, "Is everyone about done? You can keep working after our second activity, which is a game. First, count off one and two and make two teams."

The campers sorted themselves and waited.

"Okay, now each group gets five minutes to build the tallest tower you can using mini marshmallows and toothpicks. Here's a bag for each group and a box of toothpicks."

They scrambled to shove toothpicks into the marshmallows.

Hunter held up their hands. "We need a plan."

Gumball shoved three marshmallows in her mouth. "We don't need a plan. We don't care."

Soon, two leaning towers sat on the table. The first was rather spindly and the second a robust three-legged creation.

Sheila fist-bumped a teammate.

Hunter mumbled, "Told you we needed a plan."

Nikki went back to her name tag, pressing on a rainbow sticker and a peace sign.

Chapter Eight
July 18

Nikki managed to eat scrambled eggs for breakfast, then hurried to the auditorium for the morning camp meeting. She found a seat by Daniel, who was staring at his phone. She pulled hers out and scrolled to the app for the morning class options. The peer conversation sounded safer than the athletic events, although archery seemed to be compulsory.

Miranda took the podium. "We have a big day today. The morning features two sessions of archery, depending on your team color. There are several peer discussions, and a ceramics class in the afternoon. If you are so inclined, the science lab is hosting All About the Base." A thumping anthem started. "Have a good one."

After the quick message, Nikki strolled across the lobby of the auditorium.

The speakers announced, "The crafting class, More To Costumes Than Sparkle, will start in fifteen minutes in the Judy Garland room."

Nikki glanced at her phone to confirm the room number of the peer discussion and careened into McKenzie. "Sorry."

"It's okay." She opened the door. "You headed here?"

Nikki debated baring her soul in front of this woman, but then wasn't that supposed to be part of the intimacy of a friendship? And her mother was not wrong when she pointed out that Nikki could use a few more friends. She forced a smile. "Yes, thank you."

They took seats in the circle of chairs, the rest of the attendees silent.

"Good morning. I'm Chris. I use them/they. Phones away, please." Clothes rustled as electronics were shoved into pockets or bags. "Thank you. This is Exploring the Alphabet. I'll start by reviewing the current understanding of the system, and then we can share how we might fit into this range of humanity."

Daniel stood up. "This isn't the crafting class? Please excuse me."

Chris said, "Put a little sissy in that walk."

Daniel paused. "This from someone with garage doors. You got that eyeshadow all the way to your forehead."

Chris laughed and then said, "Okay, back to business. LGBTQQIP2SAA stands for lesbian, gay, bisexual, transgender, questioning, queer, intersex, pansexual, two-spirit, androgynous, and asexual."

"There is some discussion about the order of the letters, but whatever works for you is fine by me. Personally, QUILTBAG is a fun-to-say variation of the LGBTQ+ acronym. It stands for queer or questioning, unlabelled, intersex, lesbian, trans, bisexual, asexual, gay or genderqueer."

"Let's unpack this bit by bit. First, who knows someone at your school that would identify with any of those labels?"

Most of the hands went up.

"Do you identify with any of those labels?" Chris asked.

One of the campers said, "Why would we be here

if we didn't?"

"Good question." Chris looked around. "And the answer?"

"Some people are exploring their true selves, maybe trying on some labels. Hence the Q."

"Exactly. Would any of you be willing to discuss this process with someone at your school?"

McKenzie said, "Half the band is queer. We talk about it all the time."

Nikki looked over. *I guess all the high school bands have that in common. Maybe I shouldn't have quit the clarinet after a month.*

McKenzie continued. "It's an understood code. We don't out anyone to other people, especially parents."

"Not everyone feels they can trust someone yet." Chris put their hands on their knees. "But trusting your truth will stay private until you want to share it with others is a huge step in the process. The phrase 'in the closet,' while maybe old-fashioned, does imply hiding. Does it feel like you're hiding?"

"No. I mean, we're all sort of working it out for ourselves. It seems premature to share that with family that might get confused by the changes as we work through it. There are a lot of layers to unpack."

"Yes, but we can sort them into gender identity and gender attraction. Who do you understand yourself to be, and who would you be interested in dating?"

"We should be open to dating anyone."

"Let's talk about that. Who would like to share first?"

The room fell silent. Chris let them soak in their thoughts. Nikki picked at a fingernail. She sure wasn't talking about this with total strangers. Maybe it would be easier? No, saying it out loud was owning her labels, whatever they were.

They handed out notecards and pencils. They really went old school. "Here's a little exercise. Each card has a part of the QUILTBAG, and just as fast as you see the word, jot down yes, no, or maybe for yourself."

Nikki started at the first card. No, no, no, maybe. She held the pencil over the card for a moment, then scratched it out. Yes. Then she flipped it. No, no—she paused. Asexual. What did that mean again? She just hadn't met the one. Actually, she potentially had but they hadn't said anything. She wrote no, no, and then looked up. Everyone else seemed to be finished.

"Was this easy for you? Think about how you might explore the labels that spoke to you."

A dude in the back asked, "Is there a class on human sexuality?"

"Not exactly. That's one of the fun parts you get to explore on your own, with a partner, or partners. No judgment here. Thanks for participating today."

Nikki stood and hurried out of the room.

Gumball was waiting for her. "You want to go to the cafeteria?"

Nikki glanced at her watch. "Isn't there an archery class?"

"Why on earth would I want to try that?"

"What if it's one of the contests for team color competition?"

Gumball scoffed. "Let the jocks do it. I don't need you shooting me in the ass with an arrow."

Nikki considered that Gumball might have already done archery the last two years. "Come on. It might be fun."

Daniel approached them on the path and waved a Barbie Doll at them. "Look what I made."

The figure had a yellow dress with red pumps and outlandish makeup.

Nikki asked, "Can I get a hint?"

"It's a tiny Sunshine Fanta."

"She even has a tiny purse. You did a great job." Gumball grinned.

Daniel said, "I'm calling it a Scamp at Camp and taking it to the Firefly Fortress. For the little kids. Their counselor can do the thing like the Elf on a Shelf. You know, that doll some parents leave out for their kids before Christmas."

"Except it's Scamp at Camp. Got it. Here. I've got some gumballs…the doll can be playing a game or something." Gumball took a packet from her pocket.

"Excellent. I have to hurry for the next class. Ta." Daniel took the package from Gumball.

"Sashay away, darling," Nikki said. She turned to Gumball. "Did I use that right? Or is that only to use as like leave us alone."

"Beats me. He didn't seem angry, so I think you're good."

A tall redhead with muscular arms wearing a tank top and tiny shorts walked past them. "Hi, I'm Terry. You ladies know which way to archery?"

Nikki pointed. "I'm Nikki, that's Gumball."

Terry nodded and then turned down the path.

Gumball waited a few beats and then said, "Oooh. That girl's headed to archery? I'm in now."

"Stop objectifying women."

"I objectify everyone. I don't discriminate."

Nikki watched as Gumball studied the object of her new affections. "What am I? Chopped liver?"

Gumball snapped her gum. "Is Terry a she, he, or they?"

Nikki shrugged.

"Might ought to find out."

"It doesn't matter…if you're just looking," Nikki said. She stumbled when a person knocked into her.

Emily passed by, a gym bag in her hand. "Don't tell me you're headed to archery. I'm not sure I can take that much laughing."

Nikki mumbled, "Just you wait and see."

Gumball raised an eyebrow. "You and Emily been enemies a long time?"

"We used to be friends in elementary school. Now we have history."

"Good and bad?"

"No, just bad." Nikki pressed her lips together. "One time, I'd just like to get the best of her."

In a voice like Yoda, Gumball said, "Fear leads to anger, anger leads to hate."

"Hate leads to suffering." Nikki blew out a breath. "I don't think I am afraid of her."

"You don't know the power of the dark side."

"Enough. Let's channel the hate and go shoot arrows."

❧❧❧❧❧

To Nikki's relief, the arrows stacked on the table were foam and plastic. The archery area was a grassy area with large colorful blow-up barriers to hide behind. A row of targets stood under the tree line at the side of the field.

A stocky woman lifted a bullhorn to her mouth. "This is archery class. My name is Lulabelle. She/her.

Next week there will be competition games between the teams. Only six members may play on each team. The archery game is similar to dodgeball, except with these foam arrows. The main objective of the game is to tag all of the opposing players with arrows in order to eliminate them. Today we will practice with the targets and then do a short session on the field. Please put on a helmet and an arm guard. You may not go on the field without a helmet properly secured to your head."

There was a table with helmets like Nikki had used one time at paintball, black with a clear face shield, except they had visors in several colors. She only had to try two before she found one that fit. She picked up a black arm guard and adjusted the straps.

She found Gumball. "This is pretty great, right? Now let's see if we can shoot."

Gumball aimed her bow around while making lightsaber noises. "Pew, pew, pew."

Nikki rolled her eyes. "Wrong weapon."

"You have no imagination."

Lulabelle said, "You will see the barrels with the arrows in them. Do not cross between the white line and the targets. We will all collect arrows at the same time. Do not go toward the targets until I call clear. You may start to shoot as soon as you're ready."

Nikki picked up the bow and carefully adjusted the arrow. Before she could aim, an arrow hit her in the butt. She snapped her head around. "Gumball, what the hell?"

"Oops. Sorry." Gumball did not seem sorry in the least.

Nikki refocused on the target and let the arrow fly. The plastic target fell over. She glanced down the row. Plenty of arrows were landing past the targets, and some didn't even make it that far. Once her barrel was empty, she turned to see Gumball with Terry's arms around her trying to hold the bow steady. She wasn't sure why it bothered her, but it did. Immensely. Fine, she was jealous. Why, she wasn't sure. Gumball said she had a girlfriend. Nikki wished she hadn't.

When they reached the playing field, Lulabelle gave them more directions. "These center lines divide the field in half, and it is a safe zone. You may not shoot or be shot in the safe zone, and if you do, it doesn't count. At the start of the game, this is where the arrows will be laid out. When the whistle is blown, you collect your arrows, retreat to your side, and begin. You may not go to the other team's side at any point during the game. Make two lines, one on each side. This is just for practice."

Gumball asked, "How do you win again?"

"Good question. Your team must tag out all archers on the opposing team or have the most players left when time expires."

Gumball stood next to Nikki. "I hope I manage to shoot an arrow."

"I can't wait to see how this turns out." Nikki took a position to run.

"I will be the referee. It's an honor system. Don't make me dip them in paint. You can have your own strategy, but you can't shoot if you hide the whole time. Start on my whistle and stop when I blow it again."

The shrill sound startled them into action. Nikki raced to the center line and grabbed all the arrows she could carry. She took a position behind the purple blow-up and began to shoot. Until that moment, she had forgotten that Emily was also at this class. Nikki watched as Emily strode to the line approaching the neutral zone and blasted Gumball in the head with an arrow."

Gumball passed Nikki on the way off the field. "Hit that bitch so I can get back in the game."

Nikki didn't have to, as two other players from their side blasted Emily at the same time. She twisted but couldn't avoid the second arrow. Gumball made a rude gesture and scooted back onto the field behind a giant red blob. Nikki picked up several arrows from the ground and handed one to Gumball. "Let's go."

Nikki shot several more arrows and as she turned to duck, she stumbled. Emily Morgan ran past, not seeming to notice Nikki. Faker. She tripped me. Nikki took aim toward her back.

Suddenly the whistle blew.

"That didn't seem like twenty minutes," Nikki said.

Lulabelle picked up the bullhorn again. "Please put your gear on this table so it can be cleaned before the next class. Thank you for coming out, and I look forward to seeing you in future team competitions."

Nikki mumbled, "Not likely." She unbuckled the chin strap and laid the helmet down. As she was working to remove the arm guard, Emily walked past.

"Another sport you suck at."

Nikki tried to act like she didn't hear her. Besides, she was better at it than Gumball, which wasn't saying much. Hopefully some of their teammates had some skill and neither of them would have to play in a real game.

On the way back to the cabin, Gumball said, "That was kind of fun."

Nikki replied, "You couldn't hit a barn. You had Terry's arms around you to help you hold the bow the whole time."

Gumball smiled. "Yeah. She seems nice."

"What about the girlfriend?"

"What girlfriend?"

"The one you said you have at school."

"It's not serious, we play the field. And she's not here."

"You suck." Gumball was a player, and Nikki didn't want any part of that. True love on a white horse wasn't exactly "it" either, but being part of a harem was not desirable at all.

Gumball laughed. "But I don't have to swallow."

Nikki punched her arm.

❧ ❧ ❧ ❧

"Attention please." The speakers squealed. "Sorry. Just a reminder, for the Dungeon and Dragon tabletop games, the Dungeon Master prefers four players but can work with three or as many as six. Please allow two to four hours for the game. Bring snacks, a beverage, and dice. Electronic dice are acceptable. Beginners are welcome. Sign up your group today."

At dinner, Nikki spotted Emily.

Nikki put down her fork and said to Gumball, "I'm going to tell her off."

"I don't think you need to, but do you need backup?"

"Nope."

Nikki followed her into the hallway. "Hey."

Emily stopped.

Nikki said, "You didn't have to try and knock me down. I think you owe me an apology."

Emily put her hands on her hips. "I don't know

why you'd think I pushed you. I was ten feet away. It's not my fault you're clumsy. The ref didn't call a foul. I don't cheat."

"Well, it just seems like something you would do."

"That's childish."

"Exactly." Nikki stared at Emily. "Look, we aren't ever going to be friends, but when we get back to school, if you start calling me names or shoving me, I'm going to kick your ass."

Emily blinked several times. "You could try. But it won't be necessary." She stuck out her hand. "Truce?"

Nikki reached to shake her hand and Emily pulled hers back at the last moment.

"Don't touch me." She turned and walked away.

Nikki huffed. If Emily quit calling her names, maybe her friends would stop, too. That was enough. She called after her, "Just stay away from me."

❧ ❧ ❧ ❧

After dinner, Nikki snuck into the computer lab to access the internet unobserved. In the back row, she turned on the tower and monitor. After a few moments, the screen flickered the logo of Camp Iris. She opened a video chat and sent the link to Georgi. Soon her familiar face popped on the screen.

Nikki leaned in toward the monitor. "Hey, Georgi."

"Whoa. Has your mom seen your hair?"

"This girl in my cabin cut it for me."

"You don't think your mom will be mad?"

"No, I mean, so what? It'll grow. Are you alone?"

"Yes."

"I need to talk to you. Two things. First of all, Emily Morgan is here."

"No surprise."

"No, but the torture continues." She lifted her hair, showing the lump on her head. "I think she pushed me into the dock."

"You can hardly tell. How's it feel?"

"It hurts if I touch it."

"So don't touch it."

Nikki considered her next words.

"Did the screen freeze?"

"No, I was just thinking…"

"Suck it up. You didn't reach out to tell me about your bump. What's the real issue?"

"I think I like somebody."

"Not the same person who cut your hair?"

Nikki pursed her lips.

Georgi slapped her forehead. "Right, so this person is infinitely more cool than you, and somewhat more than me. Hottie?"

Nikki wiggled in the chair. "I guess. I mean, I don't know."

"Tell me three things you like about them?"

"Confident. Funny. Eyes that bore into my soul."

"You're already lost to me. I hope she isn't threatened that you have a super attractive best friend."

From the hallway, the bang of a door startled her. Nikki craned her neck. "I gotta go. I'll try and call you again."

"Sure, and for the record, you look happy. That's cool."

"Thanks." A shadow moved in front of the door and Nikki froze. She wiggled the mouse to turn off the computer, then slid toward the floor under the desk.

She waited several moments, listening for sounds of a door opening. It remained quiet. She leaned out from under the table and the hall appeared empty. She edged her way along the computer stations, eased the door open, then strolled down the hall like she owned the building. Acting like you belonged where you were was halfway to actually belonging there. She passed a janitor and nodded. The woman in the green uniform winked in return. Nikki's secret was safe.

Chapter Nine
July 19

The next morning before her alarm went off, Nikki woke to a soft nudge.

Gumball's face loomed next to her. "You won't believe it. Try and Google 'Emily Morgan athlete.'"

Nikki flicked at the screen and in moments was staring at the image of Emily in a basketball uniform.

Gumball whispered, "Just tap the picture." Immediately the screen was filled with a dozen porn sites.

"I don't understand."

"I guessed she'd have a recruiting page for colleges and that. Guess what the coaches find instead?"

Nikki giggled. "Oh my God, that's hilarious. How do we undo it?"

"We don't. But once someone on their staff becomes aware, the original site can easily break the links. I'm sure it's not the first time it's happened. It seems an obvious weak spot in their software."

"And no one can track it to you?"

"Please."

"Right. What was I thinking?"

"You might as well get up. We have a lightsaber class first thing. It might end up in the color competition. I figure we can learn that faster than field hockey or something."

Reluctantly, Nikki slid down. In the bathroom, she texted Georgi.

Revenge is sweet.
Revenge?
Google Emily Morgan
Dots flashed, then stopped. After several moments, they started again.
OMG how???
The new friend. Almost as good as you.
Can't wait to meet her
How do you know it's a her?
Duh, hair cut girl?
Yes.
U like her a lot
I guess
Give me the deets later
K bye
Nikki stuffed her phone in her pocket.

❧ ❧ ❧ ❧

After breakfast and chores, Nikki followed Gumball and Daniel to the auditorium. They settled into seats at the back near their cabin mates.

Mr. Novak danced to the podium, music blasting a heavy bass beat that vibrated the chairs. The music decrescendoed, and he said, "Another day, another slay. Good morning, campers! Today's schedule offers swim lessons in the pool and a choice of several classes including graffiti art, lightsaber technique, and beginning canoeing. Everyone is to attend the body positivity session here in the auditorium after lunch."

He cleared his throat. "Ah, yes. The persons who hung the canoe on the flagpole should remember to take off their high school sweatshirt next time. Remember, these color events are rewarded for good sportsmanship. Fifty points deducted from the Red Team."

Gumball cackled.

Nikki looked at her. "What's so funny?"

"Later."

A cloud of pink smoke started to fill the hallway as they left the auditorium.

Gumball laughed. "Either the Red Team is fired up today, or some other team is getting them in trouble."

Nikki giggled as two people with fire extinguishers blasted the color bombs as people scrambled away. "Epic."

Gumball nodded. "So now how do we outdo that?"

"I have an idea. Let's hack a code into the schedule so when people look it up, the letters all turn yellow."

"Yes. With a rainbow glitter bomb!"

"What if we get caught?"

"What if we don't?" Gumball took a set of sticky googly eyes and smacked it on a trash can.

"I saw that."

"Hilarious, right?"

Nikki noticed other sets of eyes as they walked. "You've been busy."

"I don't know what you're talking about."

"The eyes have it."

"I have a team. We start with the glow-in-the-dark ones this afternoon."

"Why?"

"Because we can." Gumball chortled. "I try to mix it up between little pranks and our larger projects."

"Did you help hang the canoe?"

"Don't be plebeian. Of course not, that was the

Blue Team."

"I thought Mr. Novak said that the Red Team did it."

"Blue Team with a sweatshirt I stole from the Red Team." Gumball cackled again. "Did you see their faces when he took points from them? Epic."

❧❧❧❧

Despite her fondness for sci-fi, Nikki decided the lightsaber class was stupid, with all the flourishes and pretend jabs. She showed her now blue forehead to the instructor and claimed a headache. She was excused immediately.

As she approached the cabin, she heard the chants of Mello Yellow. Unless there was a case of the drink in an ice cooler, she wasn't interested. She had hoped to be alone, but evidently not everyone had a class or practice this morning. Team Yellow. Could be worse, but she wasn't sure how. The other teams made comments related to yellow snow every time they announced some score or update about the competition.

She stopped and stared at the crepe paper in the trees outside their door. Red. This meant war, or more war than they already had waged. Was that a thing? No doubt Gumball had something already in the works. She slipped around the crowd and approached her bunk. With just one hand, she grabbed the frame and climbed over into the bed. She propped her arm up on a wad of blanket and closed her eyes. The chanting moved outside as the group probably had another event or something. Another ibuprofen would have been a good idea, but she didn't want to get back down.

She had just dozed off when a soft touch to her arm woke her.

Gumball's face loomed next to hers. "Do you need anything? I got you a Popsicle. Lime. They were out of grape."

"And they don't make yellow ones?"

"They didn't have any. And we aren't eating anything red."

"Correct." Gumball nodded.

"Although cherry is my favorite."

Gumball tore the wrapper, scooted the paper down toward the stick, and handed the cold treat to Nikki.

"Thanks." She bit off a piece and let the liquid tickle down her throat as she swallowed. "I do like lime. Really, I like most flavors."

"The fruit ones are gross, with little pieces of God knows what in there." Gumball scowled. "Anyway, I'm not sure how much we want to escalate this little back-and-forth."

"You're assuming she knows about the website links. She's kind of a Neanderthal. Well, no, more of a stupid Barbie. We've been at each other for years."

"Well, I don't like her being mean to you. I don't think she's stupid, though not a genius. Athletic skills are great, might even pay for college, but it fades. Your brain is forever."

Nikki thought about her grandmother with dementia, wrapped in a crocheted blanket, agitated as she tried to find the word that escaped her. She changed the subject. "What's your next class?"

"Poker. I'm asking them to add you."

"Why? I've never played poker."

"No worries. I got an app on my phone. I'll send

the link to you, and you can practice." She held up the device, swiped, and tapped the screen. "You've got until three when the next class starts. I'm headed to the shop. You get some rest."

With that, Gumball was gone and Nikki was alone in the cabin. A soft breeze whistled through the screen door. Maybe leaving all their personal stuff unattended all day was a mistake. It seemed no one—except Gumball—thought about invading privacy. Even then, she didn't take anything. Nikki tapped the screen and cards flew around. Her eyes fluttered shut and soon she was dreaming about a legion of robots chasing the Red Team across a gymnasium.

⁂

The speaker crackled to life. "Reminder, campers, you must complete the swimming test by tomorrow if you want to go in the lake during the luau Saturday night. The Green Team is making flower wreaths so we can get laid. Wait, who wrote this?"

There was a hiss and the microphone stopped. After a moment, it clicked back on.

"Also, please shower off any glitter before going into the pool. It's clogging the filters. Thank you."

Chapter Ten
July 20

Walking like a zombie, Sam from the visual arts team approached the microphone. "I usually avoid being onstage during live theater."

Laughter rippled through the audience.

"The classes today include movie makeup, which I'm teaching, and I expect many interesting characters will be at lunch. This evening is our first DJ bash at the pavilion starting at eight p.m."

Nikki rushed to the build room, her shirt sticking to her back as she walked. The humidity frizzed her hair and her feet squeaked in her flip-flops. It might be time to reconsider the number of dark items in her wardrobe. She passed by Emily in a group of girls headed the other way. Even that couldn't damper Nikki's mood, as today was the day the Yellow Team would begin the build process.

She opened the door. Stacks of Lego boxes sat on the table in the middle of the Owl's top secret building laboratory, otherwise known as Meeting Room F. Miranda, Daniel, Aaron, McKenzie, Elliot, Hunter, Asa, and Jesse all stood around Gumball.

Hunter stood with a marker in their hand in front of a whiteboard covered with stick figures in assorted poses.

Daniel, his lean frame stretched to full height, spread his arms. "Like this."

Gumball nodded. "Yes."

McKenzie scrolled through her phone. "If we can get the kits, it will save a lot of time. Does it matter if they are humanoid?"

Miranda shook her head. "That would be more like a dance team, but really anything we can get eight of would be fine."

Asa, the youngest of their team, pointed. "This one has a sort of spider look."

McKenzie said, "Eh, that has possibilities. What if we make the legs longer for height?"

Hunter shrugged. "Not sure that's important if we get the camera right. I think the drone shooting the image shouldn't be part of the display."

"Or maybe at the end it could drop something? Confetti?" Nikki said.

"I think that would be cool," Gumball said. "Can we get yellow only, or do we have to make it all the colors of the rainbow?"

Nikki sighed. "Crafts. Paper cutting. Always it's back to that."

Hunter said, "While two of you start building all the robots, Gumball should start programming, and I'll start the book with the steps they should take. Jesse, can you match the music count to the steps?"

"Of course, but is there a time limit?"

Nikki looked up from the rules sheet. "No minimum but a maximum of six minutes."

Jesse nodded. "Let's get a light show going too. You think?"

Gumball threw up her hands. "People, we have three weeks. We have to keep to a schedule in the lab. Can we get in here any time?"

"During the day, sure. But around classes. You should attend at least two events a day, besides build time," Miranda said. "Starting the last week and a half, we'll have group team competitions to participate in."

Nikki said, "Alrighty, then. Let's get back to the robot build."

McKenzie sighed. "We don't have much of a budget, so we should forget the kits. Too much money. We need probably a dozen servos for each one. Let's just use plastic pipe and water bottles."

"And wiffle balls for the head? Please," Gumball said. "I'll get my dad to pay for the kits. Will we need infrared sensors?"

"Of course, otherwise they might crash into each other," Hunter said.

Gumball snapped her bubble gum. "Or the wall, or us, or off the stage."

"I guess I better find out the dimensions of said stage," Miranda said. "Who wants to order pizza?"

"Not me. I want to see the movie makeup people are wearing at lunch," Asa said.

Hunter nodded. "Last year there were monsters and even a dude with a bullet hole in his forehead."

"No clowns?" Asa asked. "Some people really hate clowns."

"Sorry, yes. Lots of clowns."

Asa smiled. "Excellent."

※ ※ ※ ※

After lunch, Nikki sat by the fountain and spotted Emily. She had the urge to trip Emily as she marched past without speaking.

Nikki mumbled, "That's right. Just keep moving."

Emily spun around. "What is your problem?"

"You are."

"You cut your hair with a lawn mower and I'm your problem?"

Nikki ran a hand over her head. "It's cool and you're jealous."

Emily snorted. "As if." She turned to leave.

Nikki shouted, "You pushed me into the dock. You're always saying shitty things about me and I'm sick of it."

Emily stared her in the eye. "Is that what you think?"

"Yes." She held up her hair over the bruise on her forehead. "That's what I think."

Emily raised her voice. "For your information, I tried to keep you from ramming your head into the dock. I grabbed you and pushed you toward the lifeguard."

Nikki opened her mouth and then closed it. "You tripped me at archery practice."

"I did not. You tripped because you can't walk and chew gum." Emily crossed her arms over her chest. "Why do you think I'd do something like that?"

"You're always with the popular kids and say snotty things to me. Or ignore me."

"Which would you prefer?"

"I don't know. We used to be friends until third grade, and you've called me names ever since. You're a jerk."

"I'm a jerk? You were the jerk. Georgi and I were best friends. Although I didn't have words for it at the time, I really liked her. A lot. We hung out all the time until you shoved your way in and broke us up."

Nikki blinked at her for a moment.

"Never mind." Emily turned to walk off.

Nikki grabbed her arm. "Wait. You had a crush

on Georgi since elementary school?"

Emily pulled away and turned pink. "Maybe."

"So why did you call me a lesbian all the time?"

Emily practically spit out her words. "Well, you are."

Nikki's face heated with anger. "And if everyone was pointing at me, they wouldn't look at you. I think I hate you more than ever."

Emily shrugged. "Nothing new there." She hurried away, and Nikki was sure she saw Emily brush tears from her eyes.

Gumball appeared at her side and sat down. "You okay?"

Nikki nodded. "I just had it out with Emily."

"See, how revenge works, is once you do it, you just move on. Clean slate."

"It's not that easy."

"Why not?"

"History." Nikki shuffled her feet, listening to the spray in the fountain while Gumball waited. "Emily and Georgi used to be friends. She seems to think I stole Georgi from her in second grade. She's called me names ever since."

"Georgi...your gamer friend?"

Nikki nodded.

Gumball asked, "Maybe she liked her as more than a friend?"

"I guess. She admitted she kind of had a crush on her. Not that any of us had words for that kind of thing."

Gumball took a deep breath and sighed. "I'm going to go out on a limb here and say that even as a child, Emily instinctively knew not to say she liked Georgi that way. And she thought you and her were different, and as soon as you show any bit of difference from your group, you're an outsider and people dislike you. Outgroup bias. You were just collateral damage when she tried to protect herself from that bias."

"Seems to me she was just a coward."

"Maybe, but it's hard to be brave at that age and go against the grain at all, let alone defend something you don't have words for. Does it make you hate her any less?"

Nikki bit at her lip. "I kind of feel sorry for her."

"Well, just think about it. There are more of them than us. We can't afford to alienate anyone who might be an ally someday."

"Archenemy to ally. Just like that?"

"Just think about it." Gumball's phone played a melody. "I gotta go. See you later."

Nikki dipped her hand in the water behind her then splashed her face. Had Georgi abandoned Emily for her? That was the impression of an eight-year-old. Maybe they had. Did Georgi know about any of this? Probably not. She shook her hand dry and tapped a message to Georgi.

Hey R U & Emily friends?

Dots started and stopped. They started again.

We're not enemies. Gotta go.

Nikki stared at the icons on her screen. What did that mean?

Chapter Eleven
July 21

At the camp meeting, Thomas, his face and neck beet red, tapped the mic with a finger. "Today is the Big Luau on the beach, complete with a cookout. Wear sunscreen if you have outdoor games today. Do not forget your face. Little dudes, don't forget your ears."

Mr. Novak replaced him at the podium. The images switched to the schedule of activities.

"Just a reminder that there are many opportunities for peer meetings, instructional classes, craft projects, and group activities. Your team project should not be your only priority. Camp Iris is a place for personal exploration and self-reflection. If you become overwhelmed, the medical staff have counselors on staff to hear your concerns. I look forward to seeing you at the cookout tonight at the lake. The menu includes chicken, hamburgers, veggie burgers, and hotdogs. There will be additional vegetarian and vegan box meals in the cafeteria if you would prefer. Now sashay to your next event, darlings."

As they walked to their cabin, the speakers blasted. "Attention. Afternoon mediation and yoga have not been replaced with axe-throwing. Whoever placed the targets made from the trash can lids around the campus, please return them to the cafeteria. The luau starts at the waterfront at six p.m. Dinner will be served."

**

That evening, a team catered the meal and cooks with white aprons staffed huge barrel cookers with barbecued chicken, hotdogs, and hamburgers. The scent of charcoal and roasting meat wafted across the camp. Coolers of drinks sat beside long serving tables. Brightly colored serving vessels matched the decorations fluttering in the breeze. A dozen silver chafing dishes, some over ice and some over cans of burning gel, promised a feast.

Beach towels with corporate logos had been set out, and campers found spots to picnic all across the lawn. Several groups played volleyball on the sand beach. A climbing rock wall had been brought in, and there were lines at each station. In the back corner, a steel drum band wearing tropical shirts played Caribbean rhythms, and a limbo contest was in progress.

Nikki balanced her food on her lap cross-legged on the ground. Asa kicked at a hacky sack with Aaron, the small ball occasionally rolling near Nikki, Gumball, and Hunter. Miranda came by with a bag of beads and handed them all a white one with "Hang Loose" printed on it in teal. Nikki untied her lanyard, added the bead, and reattached it to her name tag.

As the sky turned tangerine over the water, sets of glowing eyes appeared in the woods behind them. Nikki wasn't sure who noticed it first, but soon the crowd was focused on the trees. Asa and some of the younger kids screamed, while Nikki and her friends laughed.

Thomas and Justin went to investigate.

Thomas yelled, "It's just a bunch of glow sticks pushed into a paper tube. No aliens, no Bigfoot."

Gumball nudged Nikki. "Amateurs. Although a Bigfoot or aliens would be pretty cool. I thought tonight's escapade might be a little lame, but not compared to this eyeball thing."

"It was kinda funny."

"Yeah. I guess." Gumball nodded toward Miranda. "And that's when I told him—oh, hi, Miranda."

"I assume this was not you?"

Gumball feigned offense. "This halfhearted attempt? Hardly."

"Do me a favor and don't get caught."

"Have I ever?" Gumball held up her drink cup. "I'm the best."

Nikki watched, curious to discover how much Miranda really knew about the prank war.

**

After the rest of the cabin had fallen asleep, Nikki and Gumball commenced Operation Balloon Drop. They had been out over an hour, and Nikki wanted to get to bed. Instead, Gumball stretched the trash bag across the doorway, holding a corner at each side of the frame. Nikki unrolled a strip of painter's tape a few inches long and then stuck it to hold the plastic. They took turns tearing more tape to secure the entire side against the doorframe. Gumball pulled the last bag from the box.

Nikki whispered, "I don't see why we are doing our own door."

Gumball shook the bag and pressed an edge to the frame. "Because if we don't, they will know we did all the others."

It appeared that Gumball didn't really plan out every detail. They had been using three bags on every door. Nikki pulled out only two and the box was empty.

They needed another trash bag. Improvising, Nikki tore the bag, and soon a long pocket was formed against the door. Gumball pulled out a balloon, stretched it, and then put it to her lips, her cheeks puffing as the air expanded the bright pink glob. Nikki thought the pink quite attractive against Gumball's skin, the color almost like gum. Like the cute pouty lips.

Nikki was distracted for a moment, then jolted into action, also blowing up a balloon. She twisted the neck into a knot, her fingers sore from dozens of balloons already completed. Carefully, she placed the balloon between the door and the plastic.

Once complete, the duo of tricksters slapped a high five.

Nikki followed Gumball around to the back of the cabin. Her shirt stuck to her back. The window they'd left open was now shut. Nikki gently touched the frame and pushed up. It didn't move.

"Now what?" Nikki squinted in the darkness, sweat starting to bead on her forehead.

Gumball tested another window. It, too, was locked.

The hours without sleep were forgotten as the panic-induced adrenaline surged. Nikki could feel her pulse in her temple. She stared at the back door. Could it really be that simple? She clutched the knob and turned.

Gumball patted Nikki's back. "Great job."

Through the dark cabin, they tiptoed to their bunk. Dropping her clothes, Nikki slid into the cool sheets, her eyes heavy as her head hit the pillow.

Chapter Twelve
July 22

The bang from the balloon as it popped woke Nikki. Hunter and Daniel were chasing them all around the cabin, stomping the balloons when they were close.

Daniel shouted, "That's five for me. Get moving, Hunter."

Miranda staggered into the great room. "What's happening?"

McKenzie stretched. "Some moron taped balloons outside our door, and when Hunter opened it, they fell all over the floor. Then they and Daniel started the pop fest."

Nikki pressed her face into her pillow to muffle the laughter.

Gumball scooted across the floor. "Watch out. Need the bathroom."

Miranda's eyes followed Gumball and then settled on Nikki. "Yeah. This is hilarious." A balloon popped and she jumped.

Nikki recovered and sat up. "Guess it's time to get up."

Miranda put her hands on her hips. "I suspect some of us have been sleeping longer than others."

"I have no idea what you mean," Nikki said.

"Tick tock, people, almost breakfast." Hunter stomped the last balloon. "That was awesome."

Miranda said, "It was something, all right."

The din in the auditorium quieted and Mr. Novak approached the lectern. "As you know, most of the staff has been awarding points this week. To keep everyone motivated, the current standings will be found on the central camp sign. Starting tomorrow, our color teams will each sign up to have a feature day, which may include any type of event including pop-up entertainment or decorations. I have gotten reports from the staff that your efforts have been fierce and many points have been awarded. Our camp staff will continue to reward campers for sportsmanship, team spirit, and general badassery. On a related topic, no tea, no shade, some of you pranksters will lose points for your team."

A voice yelled from the back, "What do the badasses win?"

Mr. Novak leaned to the microphone. "Besides eternal glory and admiration?" He smiled. "Oh, girl, do we have prizes. All mega team winners will receive a gift card to the bookstore. All color team winners will receive a Bluetooth water bottle with the Camp Iris logo, and the highest individual from each team wins a one-thousand-dollar scholarship. Can I get a gay-men?"

The room erupted into the response. "Gay-men."

Nikki walked out of the auditorium with Daniel and Gumball. Miranda caught up to them and said, "Y'all go to the build room, and I'll go see how we're doing on the point count."

A half hour later, Miranda burst into the lab carrying a box. "Good news. We are solidly in the middle of the pack. It looks like Team Red is the one to beat." She reached into the carton. "Everybody grab a T-shirt. I have a bunch of colored beads and some armbands. We're supposed to be easily identifiable as a team to the rest of camp."

Gumball said, "I can make up some hair ribbons."

Nikki snorted. "Oops, sorry. I just didn't think…"

"I know, it's a skill set you wouldn't expect from me."

Miranda continued. "And we need to decorate the cafeteria on Thursday. Posters, streamers, balloons, stuff like that."

"Arts and crafts, anyone?"

"That's your lane, Daniel," McKenzie said. "Maybe the cooks will let us dye the food."

"Or at least decorate a cake or something," Aaron said.

"Right. Maybe we should take little red wagons and make floats. Only if we can paint them yellow."

"That is an excellent idea. I'll suggest it to the other team leaders, and we can have a parade."

Nikki grinned. "With robot animatronics? I'm in."

❧❧❧❧

In the backstage dressing room, the group discussion on "Accepting Your Identity" rolled into the second hour. The lighting in the room cast a greenish glow onto everyone's faces. The couches and beanbags gave a casual feel to the space. Someone wore too much perfume, which scented the air lightly of flowers and spice. Into this seemingly peaceful space, the self-reflection on identity was difficult and scary. At least

Nikki thought so.

"I just don't know. I mean, what if I just want to be who I was really meant to be?" Hunter asked.

Chris again led this session. "You're going in circles. No one can answer that for you, and although I can validate your confusion, whatever you decide, this is a solo journey."

Nikki shifted and the bean bag dumped her sideways. Propping on an elbow, she said, "Is it a decision at all, or is it deciding to be your true self?"

Chris said, "Good point. Cis-het people just assume we made a conscious choice, and the choice was acknowledging our truth."

McKenzie put her hands on her knees. "What if there was a machine that you walked through, and it made you exactly who you are on the inside?"

Hunter folded their arms. "Like would the machine know? Or would you have to tell it, like if you wanted to transition, and you just walked through?"

"Yeah, and you could make small changes, too," Nikki said. "Like instead of needing braces, or glasses, or anything, just walk through and you're fixed."

Hunter said, "Fix a bad haircut?"

Nikki rubbed her head. "Or keep a perfect one."

"Yes! And no hormones or anything," Hunter added. "You were just you."

A low voice asked, "And at what age could you decide you could make these changes?"

Gumball said, "Back to that debate. I mean, hormone blockers just delay what people want. Why not let them transition as soon as they decide?"

"One person wishes they could go back and not transition, and the whole population is denied their right." McKenzie rolled her eyes.

Chris waited a beat. "Is it your right at thirteen? Or your parents'?"

McKenzie waved her arms. "Fine, so your parents can let you go through the machine."

A silence fell across the room as people pondered this fantastic idea.

Gumball whispered, "Or they could erase who you are and make everyone cis-het."

"Not everyone's parents would do that," Nikki said.

"What if it wasn't up to parents?" Hunter asked. "They could make a law and any little boy wearing his mother's shoes could be shoved through the machine?"

McKenzie chimed in. "Why stop there? Any kid who misbehaves is reworked."

Hunter said, "Who decides what behavior is acceptable in a society? What is fine here is not somewhere else."

Chris nodded. "Circling around on the machine idea. What if the machine could make an evaluation and then force the changes it deemed correct?"

Gumball held up a hand. "Machines only do what people make them do."

"Exactly! And what do you want them to do?"

"Get me off this hamster wheel of self-doubt," Hunter said.

"And we can allow you to do that here," Chris said. "Cross-dress and see how that feels to you. Try the imaging software in the lab and see if you find a 'look' that speaks to you and what you want to present on the outside."

Nikki asked, "What if you find out you just hate certain parts of being a girl but don't want to be a boy?"

"Like what?" Chris asked.

"Periods. Cramps."

"Try hiding a boner. It's not that great either." Hunter shrugged.

A chime went off at the back of the room. Chris said, "We have just a few moments left. Anyone have any last thoughts to share?"

McKenzie stood. "Yes. I want to say that whatever you present on the outside, it's okay. And it doesn't change who you are on the inside. Maybe your cis clothes are the costume. Maybe the gender bending is just for fun."

Nikki stood up. As the room emptied, she touched the group leader's arm. "Can I ask you something?"

Chris nodded. "Sure. I might not answer, just saying."

"Right. So what if someone presents as female, and then you get involved and find out that their, um, anatomy isn't what you thought."

"Or wanted?"

"Yeah."

"Some people say it doesn't matter, it's who they love as the person. Some people would stop the relationship. It's up to you."

Nikki scrunched her eyebrows together. "I don't want to seem judgey. I just like women."

"There's a lot to sort out here. Gender identity is another session. But let me try it this way. My grandma would say, 'Cross that bridge when you get to it.' You don't have to pre-decide every situation in your life in one day."

"I don't want to make people mad, or hurt their feelings."

"Everyone else is exploring, too. And I know we say this is a safe space, but some people will judge you for what you say." They shrugged. "Look, I love redheads. Some people don't. It might just be as simple as that. Now let's say I met a brunette; it just wouldn't click. Or it could. My dad sure has a type. Every chick he dates is a tall blonde. Every one of them. It's fine, just his thing. Maybe it's like that."

Nikki nodded. "Maybe. Please don't tell anyone I asked."

Chris crossed their heart. "Safe space." They held out their fist.

Nikki bumped it and stepped into the hall.

❧❧❧❧

The music began to play on the phone, interrupting her nap, and Nikki blinked her eyes open then shut them again. Her head pulsed with the beat. Maybe she could get out of the next class. What did she sign up for…making potion bottles or the leather work? She hadn't worn a belt in years, so leather was out. A soft voice startled her.

Aaron touched her arm. "Hey, are you awake?"

Nikki nodded and opened her eyes.

"Gumball asked me to come check on you. We all have the Potion Bottle Brewing class."

Nikki sighed. What the hell was she going to do with the bottle? Maybe Aaron would want a set. "Thanks, buddy. I'm looking forward to it."

She slid down. They walked together to the craft center. A group of people dressed in cloaks dashed past them. She wasn't sure if they were headed to do some live action role-playing game or had finished a sewing class. Either would have been better than the bottle class. Aaron was jiggling one foot as they waited. Nikki recognized the tall, slender person who was instructing as the mysterious Sam from the Green Team. Artists and actors. Was she attracted to the androgyny? It seemed not.

Gumball slid into an empty seat at their table just as the instructor started the class.

"Hi. I'm Sam. I'm with the Porpoises. The Green Team." They brushed back long hair. "We'll be making potion bottles today. There are a lot of ways you can go about this project. First, you each can select up to six glass containers."

Nikki glanced over at the table covered with clear jars of assorted shapes: some like a jelly jar, canning jars, round, square, skinny necks, and some with handles.

"You can mix and match, or do all the same," Sam said. "Then there is paper in the corner. This is for the labels. Eye of newt. Whatever you want. After you create the label, I have decoupage to glue them on the glass. This takes a while to dry, so be careful."

Gumball nudged her. "Eye of Emily."

Nikki whispered, "Shh."

Sam held up a finished bottle. "There are lots of corks, so find one that fits your container. Once the bottle is full, you pop on the cork and wrap it with the twine and…tada! A potion bottle."

Sam set a large box on the table. "These are plastic props you can put in the jars. Assorted fingers, toes, eyeballs, little frog parts. You don't have to use any if you don't want. To make the liquid, you have a choice of water, vegetable oil, or honey. You can add some food coloring if you like, or some glitter. There are several colors, but I'd go for the smaller particles. They float better."

Aaron wiggled in his seat. "This is sick."

Nikki smiled. She might keep hers after all. She hadn't given any thought to the project but went with a matched set of jars. She selected several eyeballs and a finger, then picked up some honey. After carefully creating the labels, some in black, some in parchment, she brushed the glass and centered the paper.

She looked over at Aaron, who was already adding glitter to his colored water rainbow set. Gumball was still drawing scrolls around a label. Nikki went back to her jar, considering the color for the bottles without a prop.

Sam cleared their throat. "Time flies when you're having fun. We have about fifteen minutes to finish and clean up. I have cardboard boxes for you to carry your jars. There's some packing paper to cushion them. Be careful of the labels."

Nikki placed her jars into a box, scrunched some paper, and arranged it around the glass.

Aaron said, "Nikki, your jars are wicked."

She smiled. "You can have them all, if you want."

Gumball nodded. "Mine, too."

Aaron grinned. "Thanks. I'm going to have a whole set on my bookshelf. Wait until my mom sees them."

Nikki winked. "I'm sure she will be speechless."

"Or I'll turn her into a frog." Aaron waved his hands in the air.

Gumball said, "You might need a wand for that."

Aaron frowned. "You're right. I wonder why we don't have a wand class?"

Nikki nudged Gumball. "Probably so we don't turn our parents into frogs."

Chapter Thirteen
July 23

In the morning, dressed like the Blue Man Group, the Blue Team had several members greet everyone at the cafeteria doors. The music group was in full force with streamers and blue confetti covering the tables in the cafeteria. In the corner of the room, a string quartet played a muted version of an Ed Sheeran song, the bass player bouncing on the heels of his feet in a counter rhythm to his beat. Each of them had on a blue T-shirt streaked with white in a tie-dye swirl.

A group in matching shirts marched into the room, each holding strings attached to balloons. They tied them to chairs and handed them out to fellow campers. The Blue Men appeared with drums and added a crazy pattern to the music. A conga line formed, and students leaped to join, shuffle, shuffle, shuffle, and kick. Twisting around the tables, they danced, feet kicking out at random times, whistles rising above the din.

Mr. Novak entered the room and the line circled around him. He clapped his hands in delight. "Wonderful. A hundred points to the Blue Team and fifty to everyone else for participation. Someone give them all beads. Carry on."

Nikki accepted the blue bead with a music note on it, then strung it onto her name tag.

After the camp announcements at the morning meeting, Nikki and Gumball hurried to the build room for the robotics project. They had asked for extra tables to be installed for assembly space. The scent of plastics greeted them as they pushed into the now crowded room. In the overly air-conditioned space, goose bumps popped on Nikki's arms. Miranda handed Nikki a notebook for her record keeping. An entire pallet covered in shrink wrap stood in the corner.

Gumball took a pair of scissors and cut the plastic covering. "Okay, everyone tell Nikki which parts you are going to unpack and inventory so we can get a count. If anything seems broken, we need to reorder right away."

After an hour and a half of tearing open packaging and tallying contents, Nikki announced, "That's everything." She looked over at the tables. Everything was in labeled boxes. "And thank goodness Daniel has sick organizational skills or we wouldn't find anything."

Gumball started the clapping. After a few moments of cheering, she put up her hands and the room fell quiet. "And now we start the build. Instead of an assembly line, how about each of us build one at the same time? Miranda can pass out parts as Nikki reads the directions."

Miranda cracked her knuckles. "I'm ready."

The team barely noticed the announcement over the intercom. "Attention campers and swim enthusiasts. The Merpeople Swimming Challenge has been delayed until two thirty p.m. due to a schedule conflict with the Drag Makeup for Beginners session. Again, Merpeople Challenge at two thirty today."

Chapter Fourteen
July 24

After the morning meeting, Hunter fist-bumped Nikki. "Today, we have an adventure."

"As long as we don't have to wear cloaks," Nikki said. She patted her pocket to confirm her bag of multisided dice was still in place.

They feigned offense with a hand to their chest. "I just had mine laundered especially for today."

A tall guy with the beginnings of a mustache walked past their table. Hunter watched him with interest.

Nikki smiled at Hunter. "Dude, go talk to him, and I'll see you at the game."

Hunter brushed their hair back with one hand. "Thanks." They scooted after the young man.

Nikki and Gumball followed the signs in the game room to the D and D table. A tall person with long dark hair hunched over a tablet, tapping furiously. She looked up and waved a hand. "Take a seat, I'm Nyssa and I'll be the Dungeon Master this fine day. Have a snack, get comfortable. I have a character sheet for each of you already printed. Does everyone have dice?"

Hunter flew into the room. They flopped next to Nikki. "I have dice and a phone number."

Nyssa looked over at them and continued. "We'll be having an adventure called 'The Wild Sheep Chase,' and it's available online for free from the Dungeon

Masters Guild."

Nikki poked Gumball. "I hope you're not the sheep."

"No one will be a sheep, at least in the context of this game." Nyssa brushed her chestnut hair from her face. "Each character has a description of what they are like, and the numbers at the top will affect the success or failure of any action you take. For instance, if you spit on a dragon and have no shield, you will die instantly."

"Shit." Gumball glanced at Nikki. "This may be a short game."

"Just a point, there are healing potions. I won't kill any of you off the first hour." Nyssa winked. "And if you all pick to be an elf, it will take until midnight with all the NPCs I'll need to bring."

Nikki whispered, "Non-player characters."

"I know," Gumball said.

"Really?"

"No, I have absolutely no idea what that means."

⁂

After a long role-playing session, Gumball kicked at the dirt as they strolled across camp. "I don't know why I had to be the freaking human. I spent the whole game unconscious or being carried around by the sheep."

Nikki shrugged. "You could have been the dwarf or that dragon thing."

"I can't believe the sheep had to rescue me. Twice."

"Well, Nyssa was trying to keep you alive."

Hunter came up behind them. "Excellent

adventure, my fellow Yellow Team compadres. I'll be late for the build, but I'll be there. I'm meeting somebody."

Nikki fist-bumped him. "I hope the same somebody from breakfast."

"Yep." They hurried up the path.

❧❧❧❧

When they walked into the build lab, McKenzie and Daniel were shoulder to shoulder over a table.

Nikki said, "Hi. Qué pasa?"

Daniel held up a small figure. "We made toppers out of fondant for our color day in the cafeteria."

She looked over his shoulder. Tiny computers and mini keyboards were in rows. "Excellent. You must have dozens."

"Actually, a hundred and twenty-five," McKenzie answered. "We're going to have cupcakes with yellow frosting from the kitchen. Miranda already asked the cooks. Then we'll decorate them with these."

"That should be worth a ton of points," Gumball said. "Let's go eat. I'm starving. Our game took all day."
**

As the Yellow Team builders walked to the cafeteria, a steady clicking of heels on the sidewalk echoed across the courtyard. A line of students in matching red shirts marched single file to the center surrounding the fountain. They shifted into two lines and began a series of steps and hops while clapping and shouting.

Nikki had almost forgotten that the dancers were included with the athletes in the Red Team. Inside the dining hall, the tables all had red tablecloths and red balloons floated from a centerpiece made from a stone painted red. Nikki smirked. The Neanderthals used rocks to decorate.

As they ate, six members of the Red Team walked to the front of the room, each carrying a jar of mayonnaise. Justin announced, "Anyone want to challenge us to an eating contest?"

No one budged.

"Fine. We'll race ourselves. Whoever finishes first wins a camp sweatshirt."

They each twisted off the lid, accepted a spoon, and waited.

"Three, two, one."

The campers screamed and gagged as the contestants gobbled the condiment. The first to finish held up his jar.

Justin said, "Well done, Ryan."

Nikki stared. Gumball nudged her. "I bet it was frosting or something in those jars."

"Really?"

"I'm sure of it."

Chapter Fifteen
July 25

Nyssa adjusted her multicolor shirt over the waist of her long red skirt and then leaned toward the microphone. "Greetings, campers. Today there are some great classes. We have a guest teacher from the Comedy Club for the improv class. There's a schedule change. Due to an incident in the chemistry lab, the science program for today is changed to Rock and Rock. Remember, tomorrow the Color War competition will move on to the next round: breakouts. These are team competitions. Sign up for the events, and captains make sure you assign alternates. Remember, each camper must compete in five breakout events. Thank you."

Miranda led Gumball and Nikki toward the building for the tabletop gaming session, circling the sports fields. Cheers rose from the softball diamond where players hopped from base to base in a strange kickball game using a two-foot rubber ball. At the pool, a cluster of swimmers in the water circled a raft, potentially trying to synchronize their movements. They nailed it—assuming it was an octopus having a square dance.

Nikki said, "Miranda, we haven't practiced anything like that."

"It's not doing them much good, is it? I'm kidding. Look, we can't be ready for everything they might throw at us. Just do your best."

Gumball added, "And win."

"Exactly. Win." At the gaming room, Miranda opened the door. "You two go ahead."

"You're not playing?" Nikki asked.

"I just got a text that we're having a meeting about camper behavior with Mr. Novak. It seems the pranks are escalating." She gave them a stern look and then smiled. "The canoe was epic, though, right?"

Gumball winked. "Epic except they got caught. Amateurs."

Nikki could feel the heat moving up her cheeks. "Bye." She grabbed Gumball's arm and pulled her into the room.

There were perhaps a half dozen tables around the room, and most had campers setting out the components of various board games. At one table, a person sat shuffling cards.

Nikki pointed to the TV monitor. "There's our people."

McKenzie and Daniel already had a game started. A person from the Blue Team stood.

"Hey, I'm Tony. Musician and gamer."

Gumball shook his hand. "Glad to meet you."

Daniel handed them each a controller. "You two are late. Should we wait in case anyone else is coming?"

Nikki shook her head. "They can go play Life or something."

Tony asked, "Does everyone know how to play?"

They all said, "Yes," in unison.

"Just checking. Ready, set, go."

Daniel laughed. "It's okay if you're all trash. They call it a garbage can, not garbage cannot. Let's do this."

Nikki furiously clicked her controller, spinning her character around as the avatar ran across the screen."

Tony pumped his arm. "Yes!"

McKenzie said, "Ever consider baseball? You're catching every fireball I throw."

Gumball furiously clicked the controller. "Gee, Mac, you should let your chair play. At least it knows how to support someone."

The screen flashed *Game Over.*

They all cheered. "Great game," Daniel said.

Tony said, "Maybe we can play again."

"I hope so, that was fun." Gumball shook Tony's hand again. "Nice to meet you."

❧ ❧ ❧ ❧

The hallway was empty, so Nikki stepped into a classroom doorway. The speakers startled her.

"Attention please. The class on Chain Mail for Cosplay will be starting in fifteen minutes in the crafting area B."

Nikki glanced around the area to confirm she was alone, then tapped her phone and waited. "Hi, Mom. How're you?"

"Oh, same old, same old. Casey just left for camp, but she'll be back before you are. Are you having a good time?"

"Yeah." Nikki paused. "I just wanted to thank you."

"Whatever for?"

"The camp thing. It's been great."

"Not as great as you are, Nikki."

"Look, I gotta go. Love you."

"Love you more."

Nikki tapped the screen and stared at the phone.

Had her mother really figured out she was a lesbian…queer…sapphic…any of those…before she had? Maybe Nikki always felt a little different, but how could Mom have known? It must have been the GI Joe.

ॐ ॐ ॐ ॐ

After nightfall, Nikki and Gumball snuck toward the gymnasium. The way Gumball had explained it, this prank was better planned, in Nikki's opinion. She stepped into the shadow by the door and waited, the pool noodles in her arms between her body and the wall. Gumball stood almost against her, the heat of her skin perceptible in the slight breeze of the night air. The drone of insects covered the noise of their breathing. Assured the world around them was still, Gumball eased open the door, and they scooted into the dark hallway. In the glow from the exit signs, they moved toward the locker room.

Gumball began lifting locker handles to locate the unlocked cubicles. Finding the first, she rummaged until she found shoes and a pair of stretch pants. She handed these to Nikki and continued her search.

Nikki carried the first set of decoys to the bathroom stall. At the back, she set the shoes on the floor. With a package knife, she cut two-foot-long sections of pool noodle. Shoving one into each pant leg, she started to giggle.

Gumball startled her. "James Bond, you are not."

"Sorry, this just cracks me up." Nikki arranged the pants on the toilet seat and stuck a leg into each shoe. She locked the stall and slid on the floor under the door. "What do you think?"

Gumball leaned down. "It's pretty good." She

handed Nikki another set of clothes.

They repeated their process until all twelve stalls appeared to be occupied. A squeak from the hallway echoed against the tile. They froze. The noise moved closer and closer to the door. Nikki held her breath as a fine sheen of moisture beaded on her lip. A lone mosquito buzzed around her ear, taunting her to swat it. The heat from Gumball's arm against her was hot and sweaty, but she smelled like sun lotion and pizza. Nikki would like to know if she tasted like pizza. The fear in her stomach changed to butterflies. Did Gumball feel the same way? She'd never hinted at more than friendship. The squeak stopped, and they heard the whoosh of water from the janitor's closet.

Nikki looked frantically for a hiding spot, but aside from squeezing into a long locker, there was none. The water stopped. Someone started to whistle, and the squeak moved farther away.

Gumball whispered, "Good to know they actually mop. Let me peek, and then let's vamoose."

Nikki nodded. Gumball leaned out the door, then waved her hand. Together they dashed down the hall and out into the night. They kept running all the way past the cafeteria.

At the water fountain, Gumball stopped, bent over, and gasped for air. "I should have tried harder in gym class."

"You mean health and fitness?"

"Call it whatever you want. It's gym class."

The spray of the fountain was stopped at night, but cool blue lights accented the water in the darkness. The temptation was great.

Nikki pushed off her shoes. "Care for a dip?"

Gumball raised an eyebrow. "That's against the

rules." She held her expression for a few moments before bursting into laughter. She kicked off her shoes and stepped into the water.

At once the moment was intimate but also potentially very public. Nikki watched as Gumball waded around, lightly swirling the water with her fingertips, her unshaved hair hanging in her eyes. Nikki realized her mouth was open and clamped it shut. Reluctantly, she stepped out of the water. With some effort, she got on her shoes.

"I'm afraid to ask what's next," Nikki said. "I almost fell asleep during the video game."

Gumball shrugged. "We can skip a night before the next event."

Nikki nodded. "That's a good idea. Throw them off our scent."

"I'm not too sure they're even looking for us. The Red Team is pretty sloppy in execution."

At the closest cabin door, a counselor stood at the window.

Nikki whispered, "Uh-oh."

Gumball waved and then climbed the steps. "Hi, Nyssa. I'm sorry we were out late. I couldn't resist the temptation of the fountain."

Since both their shorts were damp at the top, this was obvious. Better to plead to half the crime.

"Right. The pool and an entire lake aren't enough water. Get to bed."

The girls hurried past Nyssa toward their dark bunkhouse.

Chapter Sixteen
July 26

After just a few hours of sleep, the first alarms started to go off at seven. Nikki grabbed her blanket and pulled it over her head.

Gumball nudged her. "Eat your Wheaties this morning. After class is a camp meeting and then the team competitions start."

"Goodie." Nikki pulled the blanket down. "Do you want to go to Quadball on the hockey field, or Live Action Role-Playing?"

"Running around with a deflated volleyball is ridiculous."

"And exhausting."

"Right. And while LARPing has piqued my interest, I think I'll skip the land of make-believe medieval forests brimming with mythical creatures. I have something I have to do." Gumball patted Nikki's arm. "I'll see you at the camp meeting." Then she was gone.

Nikki listened as the other campers got ready for the day. It was odd that Gumball didn't at least tell her where she was going. After all, they had done everything together the whole time. Maybe she had some prank planned. No, that didn't make sense. It was daylight, plus they'd done the locker room last night. What could Gumball be up to? Nikki tapped her phone and opened the day's schedule, hoping for better options. After breakfast was LARP and Quadball, then the all-camp meeting, then team races—which all sounded terrible. Nikki tossed her phone down and tumbled from the bunk. She caught her balance and stood upright. Maybe they would have waffles at breakfast. Otherwise, this day would suck. It was off to a horrible start already.

In the auditorium, Mr. Novak said, "Good day. I hope you have enjoyed Camp Iris so far."

The campers cheered.

"Welcome to day one of the Color War tournament, where we have direct competition between our teams. Campers, as a reminder, these events highlight all the amazing strengths and abilities your team may have. During the week, players must represent their team at least once in each category. There will be brain busters, athletic challenges, full team competitions, and the performance Showcase.

"Most events will be single colors head-to-head in the challenge, either in small groups or with the entire team. For a variation, this year we are going to have mega teams for certain events, where individual teams will be combined to compete together. Reminder, the members of each color team are required to compete in at least five events over the course of the week. Check your app to see which mega team your primary color team will join."

Lights from phones glowed around the dim auditorium. Nikki quickly scrolled down to confirm that yellow was with blue and orange. Together, they were brown. Actually, red and green made brown too. Interesting. Not exactly a power color like red, was it? At least the mega team was large—that was better. The musicians weren't likely to be any better at sports, but they were sometimes pretty nerdy and should be a great addition to their team for brain busters.

He continued. "Okay, campers. At lunch, please sit with your color team to begin creating cheers for this afternoon's relay races. We start promptly at one down by the soccer field."

Justin walked to the microphone. "Please remember to wear athletic shoes. The relay races might include stations ranging from leapfrog to a three-legged-race, or even water brigade bear run."

Nikki groaned. He had to be kidding, but maybe he wasn't.

❧❧❧❧

After lunch, Nikki stood at the edge of the soccer field wearing a yellow bandanna around her neck. Relay races—how hard could that be? The plastic tubs should have been a clue that there was more to this challenge than a shuttle from one end to the other, then tagging teammates.

Gumball arrived just as Miranda began handing out spoons. "Ice cream eating relay?"

Nikki shrugged. "I'm not eating pistachio. That's all I'm saying."

Miranda said, "No, we're not eating anything. You won't have to spit out your gum, although it might be a good idea. Since it's not allowed."

"Even outdoors?" Gumball blew a bubble and snapped it.

"No. You're incorrigible. At least stop blowing bubbles." Miranda turned her attention when the speaker squeaked.

Through the megaphone, Justin announced, "I will be this afternoon's referee. At the far end of the field are totes filled with water. You may only use two spoons and only one person can be on the field at any time. The team that brings the highest amount by volume to this side of the field wins."

"I'm glad these are soup spoons," Gumball said.

They took a place on the yellow line. Considering the group's overall athleticism and graceful nature, they were doomed.

Daniel, the first racer, took his mark, the spoons clutched in his hand.

Justin held up his hands. "Wait, wait, wait. I forgot. Cue the music." A thumping dance tune blared across the field. "That's better. Since we have no purses at this race, I hope that Bob The Drag Queen will forgive me when I say, 'Spoons first, everyone.' On your mark, get set. Go." He pushed the button on an air horn, the shrill pitch startling the runners into motion.

As the race progressed, it turned out the speed some teams had approaching the water bins did not translate into an agile trip walking toward the catch basins. The Blue Team members who were members of the marching band had a strong advantage as they glided back, shoulders high, spoons held still.

Nikki cheered as Gumball dumped in her spoonfuls.

Gumball put her hands on her knees, gasping for breath. "Did he say how long we do this for?"

Nikki shook her head. "I don't think so." She put one foot forward at the line, ready to start the moment McKenzie returned. "Ha. The Red Team dude just lost his spoonfuls and now they're arguing if he gets another turn."

"Go, Nikki." Daniel nudged her.

Nikki ran across the field. With a careful scoop, she filled the spoons and then used her best imitation of a marching stride to reach the fill bucket.

Gumball clapped her on the back. "I'd say you did a good impression of a band nerd. That was awesome."

Back and forth, with speeds between walking and running, the contestants crossed the field. To be honest, it was hard to tell how they were doing, and Nikki eyed the other team bins with suspicion.

The air horn startled them. "Racers may finish this lap, and then the officials will judge the water collected."

It was no surprise that the Blue Team had the most water, but Nikki was shocked that they had come in second place. She could hear Emily arguing that there was no way the artists had beat them, but the Red Team sat in fourth place. The Porcupines, in matching neon orange shirts, seemed nonplussed by their last place showing.

McKenzie tapped Nikki's shoulder. "I'm not sure what fresh hell is next, but the Red Team is all stretching over there."

Nikki had a particularly splendid view of Emily's butt until Gumball stood in front of her.

Gumball followed her gaze. "Don't let the hate pull you down. Let it bubble up into your power. The dark force is strong."

Nikki made a swoop as if she had a lightsaber. "And they have cookies."

The team walked toward the snack tables. Nikki considered the offerings: fruit slices, chips, or cookies. Water filled a dozen paper cups. A counselor was holding a two-liter bottle of Coke.

"You want some?"

The counselor turned the top. A geyser of foam sprayed from the bottle. splashing everyone near the cookies and drinks. The same thing happened with the next bottle.

Gumball looked around and then touched Nikki's sleeve. "Notice anything strange?"

Nikki looked around. "No."

"None of the Red Team is at the snack station. They set this up."

"How'd they manage that?"

"I'd guess Mentos tied in the lid. White string. Twist and it falls, and boom."

Nikki reached for a napkin. "Pretty funny."

"Middle school stuff."

Emily came over. "Any Coke left?"

Gumball smiled. "Nice try. Thanks for playing."

Emily folded her arms across her chest. "I'm sure I don't know what you mean."

"You're outgunned. Give up."

Emily winked. "Never."

❦❦❦❦

Miranda startled Nikki as she approached the cabin after dinner. "Sorry. You are a skittish thing, aren't you? Hey, I need a little favor. The other senior counselors and I wanted to get ice cream for our cabins, and of course we can't get caught breaking the rules. Will you head over there, and when Thomas whistles, go in and get a couple boxes?"

Nikki nodded. "Call me Bond. Jane Bond." She hummed a theme song as she turned and crept back toward the cafeteria. Under the evening lights, bugs flew around the glow. She spotted a guy from the Blue Team who lived in another cabin.

He waved her over. Holding up his high-tech black wristwatch, he said, "Should be any minute now."

Emily strolled up to them. "Operation Cooldown?"

He laughed. "I wish I had thought of that. Anytime now."

Emily looked to Nikki. "How's the forehead?"

She seemed sincere. Nikki shrugged.

He asked, "What happened to your face?"

Nikki felt the heat rise up her neck as her anger at Emily rose. A simple, *she pushed me* would be enough, but nothing clever came to mind.

Emily said, "You should see the other guy." She had the nerve to wink at Nikki.

A wolf whistle sounded and Emily took the lead to the cafeteria doors. She stepped into the dark entryway, keeping one hand on the door until they had walked through. "So, who knows where the cooler is?"

He stepped forward. "My parents own a restaurant. Been working there since I could reach a table. Kitchens are all about the same. Follow me."

Nikki hesitated and Emily went right behind him. Nikki clenched her teeth as Emily's shoes squeaked on the highly polished tiles. Sweat made her shirt cling to her. They didn't seem nervous at all. Maybe she was overreacting. But then, why had the counselors sent them? The cooler door popped as it opened. She hurried in behind them.

The fan blew frosty air and a thermometer read minus ten degrees Fahrenheit. Floor-to-ceiling shelves were packed with labeled boxes of beef patties, beef tips, and assorted chicken parts. At the rear was a stack of ice cream in tubs and then the cartons of individual treats.

"I'm taking a box of ice cream sandwiches and Nutty Buddy bars." He selected his cartons.

Emily reached and pulled out two boxes of Brown Cow ice cream bars.

Just as Nikki touched the carton of Heath bars, he laughed and slammed the door as he ran out.

Emily spun around. "What a jerk."

Nikki felt the air close in around her. They were trapped. Just her and her archenemy. She'd seen all the movies. They could freeze to the floor if they didn't run out of air first.

"Have you ever worked in a kitchen?" Emily asked, her breath forming a cloud as she spoke.

Nikki shivered. "No, my dad wants me to concentrate on my studies."

"How's that working out?" Emily paused. "So you don't know how to get out?"

"No. For the record, I do wish had stayed friends. Or at least not enemies."

"Fine."

"Let me call someone." Nikki stared at the screen, now in emergency-only mode."

"Don't. We'll get in trouble."

"We're already in trouble."

"Maybe, but not because we're trapped. Look." Emily stepped aside and pointed to a button with glow-in-the-dark paint. "Emergency exit release. Plus, I bet the handle works."

Nikki let out a sigh. "Oh, thank God."

Emily cackled. "You really did think we were going to freeze?"

"Of course not, I mean, someone would have missed us and come to get us out." Nikki wasn't nearly as confident as she sounded.

Emily pulled the lever and the door swung open. "Come on, before they really do think something happened to us."

Nikki marched in silence toward the senior cabins.

The other ice cream thief hollered, "There you are."

"Nikki dropped her cigarettes," Emily replied.

Nikki hissed, "I don't smoke."

"So now you do," Emily whispered. "You want him to think we panicked? Well, at least you panicked. Not me."

Nikki squinted. Emily was covering for her, even if she had messed with her some. Gumball's words about needing allies echoed in her head. "Thanks."

Emily turned toward her cabin without another word.

Gumball raced out to meet Nikki. "Where have you been? The other cabin has been posting pics with ice cream on Snapchat for ten minutes."

"Um…see…never mind. I'll tell you later, take these inside." Nikki leaned over with her hands on her knees, the adrenaline still surging in her veins. Camp was going to kill her. After her breathing slowed sufficiently, she strolled inside.

Chapter Seventeen
July 27

On the way to breakfast, Nikki noticed a crowd gathered near the outdoor amphitheater. Evidently the Green Team was working on a project. On the stage, a dozen people in lime-colored unisuits posed in varied positions, some sitting and some standing. The other students in green T-shirts wrapped them with clear plastic wrap and tape.

Nikki watched as they worked. None of the models moved even as they wrapped carefully around their heads, avoiding their mouths. A student came with scissors, and they cut out the first finished clear mummy. Several students pulled off the form and held it as the cutter switched to package tape to secure the sections closed. They attached string to each newly formed clear body. At each post, they lifted a sculpture as high as they could reach. Another student furiously looped the string. When they were finished, the clear bodies were arranged around the space in an eerie group sculpture and the result was captivating.

❧❦❧❦

After breakfast, the counselors pushed back several of the tables and adjusted chairs to create an open space.

Mr. Novak, dressed in a casual outfit of jeans and a cotton shirt, held up his hands. "Good morning.

As usual, our teams have all used many cheers to start off our relay events for the start of direct competition between the teams. I invite each team to select their favorite for our cheer-off, and then points will be awarded."

The musicians and singers of the Blue Team made rows like a choir. One person blew a pitch pipe.

"My father is a fireman, he puts out fires, Hmmm.

"My mother is a fireman, she puts out fires, Hmmm.

"My brother is a fireman, he puts out fires, Hmmm.

"My sister is a fireman, she puts out, Hmmm."

Mr. Novak cleared his throat. "Frat row called. They want their songbook back. Let's remember to keep this rated G."

The Orange Team wandered toward the center stage. "Step back, take notes. We'll take the show and run. Forget all the other color teams, we're number one."

Gumball whispered, "That is so lame my high school cheerleaders use that one."

The entire Red Team lined up and the dancers choreographed a routine with vigorous steps and kicks. "We're R-E-D red H-O-T hot. You can't beat the team we got. We're on fire, red hot." They put their hands on their butts. "Sssss."

The audience snapped their fingers and hissed as well.

For all the creative artists in the group, the Green Team went simple. "Go Big Green. Go, go Big Green," they cheered, then stomped twice.

As they started it over for the third time, Mr. Novak interrupted. "I think we get the idea."

Nikki and Gumball went to the back to follow McKenzie, who had a knack for cheering. "Hey, hey you. Get out of the way. Today's the day. We blow you away." They raised their hands and blew a kiss to the crowd.

The camp counselors and staff all jogged onto the stage wearing yellow wigs and T-shirts with letters on them that spelled SUNSHINE. And the campers went crazy cheering.

"R-O-W-D-I-E, that's the way we spell rowdy, rowdy. Let's get rowdy."

As they started a second time, Mr. Novak joined them. Soon everyone was standing and yelling.

He took the bullhorn offered to him. "That was fantabulous. You may sashay away to your next team events. Basketball in the gym, Mojo Kickball in the back field, Trivial Pursuit in the game room. Pick up your rainbow bead at the door as you leave. Thank you."

✿ ✿ ✿ ✿

Nikki adjusted the strap to her backpack. "Remind me again why we're playing basketball the first round?"

"Simple. Mind games. At the beginning we lull them into thinking we can't win. At sports, we will get cremated, then we hit them hard at the cerebral challenges. We'll conquer all and race to the top. Besides, I bet the points get higher, and we will lose less than on the early competitions."

Gumball opened the gym door and heard the squeaking shoes mixed with shouts of directions. Hunter and Asa sat on a bench. The Red Team players had matching basketball uniforms, unlike the Yellow Team members, who looked like they all pulled clothes from a laundry basket.

Nikki whispered, "We are going to be murderized."

Of course, Emily was there, her arm muscles flexing as she shifted the ball, looking for a player to pass it to.

Hunter took two steps onto the floor before the ball hit them on the side of the head.

"Nice catch, loser." A tall girl in a red uniform grabbed the ball and ran back across the gym.

Gumball picked up Hunter's glasses. "We're off to a great start. They'll really underestimate us now."

Hunter accepted the glasses, inspected the frames, and then propped them on their face. "Yeah, they look really scared."

The Red Team ran in a crossing pattern down the floor, the ball snapping between them until a giant slammed it into the basket.

Gumball shrugged. "We're so low, we can steal the ball right out from under them."

Nikki mumbled, "Getting crushed under them is what I'm afraid of."

Gumball smiled. "Alright, champs, let's warm up."

The unskilled friends took turns lobbing the ball toward the rim, and a few times it came close to a basket.

Several people wearing yellow approached. McKenzie's hair was now a bright purple. "Hey, fellow lemonites. Ready for death by exertion?"

Jesse, whose hair was spiked into a faux-hawk, stretched their arms out. "I was born ready."

Nikki managed a basket. "Oh yeah, we got this."

She danced around in a circle.

Gumball slapped her a high five. "I like the attitude."

Nikki glanced across the room at the Red Team, now stretching, the fabric tight over their bodies. "Who's that by Justin? He must be seven feet tall."

"Who cares? But for the record, he's Ryan. He goes to my school. He plays football and basketball." Gumball grabbed her left shoulder with her right hand, her neck popping as she twisted.

"Of course he does." Nikki watched as Emily pulled her arms over her head, her chest pushing out. Nikki felt dizzy as the blood left her brain.

Sam, a camp counselor with the art and actors team, wore a striped shirt. He approached the group. "Do you have enough to play?"

"Enough what?" Gumball asked.

"People." He shook his head. "This is going to be sad."

Fifteen minutes later, Sam's prediction came true. The score was twenty-six to four. Gumball tried to steal the ball, or at least that's what it looked like. Nikki held her breath as Gumball spun in front of a Red Team member, caught the edge of his shorts, and tugged, a nice set of rainbow compression shorts coming into view. The ref blew the whistle and was arguing with a member of the Red Team about the penalty.

Gumball was face to chest with the tallest red player. "Bam. How'd you like another?"

Nikki grabbed her arms and pulled her back. "You are going to get us killed."

The Red Team huddled around the ref, the gestures indicating a heated discussion.

Finally, he handed the ball to Emily to throw it

in. She snapped the ball toward their basket and ran onto the court.

As Nikki tried to block Emily, she caught her foot. In slow motion, her body tipped forward, arms swinging like a windmill, until her knees made contact with the wooden floor and then she did a face-plant. Her left hand slapped off the smooth surface. She froze to assess her pain level before she got up. Sitting, she touched her face, but it seemed she hadn't broken her nose. Her hand throbbed but looked okay. Two hands grabbed her from behind. She pushed up and stood, brushing her elbow. "Thanks."

Gumball said, "She's next."

Nikki shook her head furiously. "No. Stop antagonizing them. Let's just run out the clock and get the heck out of here."

Two teammates ran past, Hunter dribbling with a full palm. After three more steps, they attempted a layup, jumping toward the basket. The ball banged off the backboard, hit the front of the rim, and by some miracle bounced back into the net.

Hunter cheered. "Simple physics. Stop trying to be fancy. We got this."

Nikki shook her head. She panted, unable to speak.

The Red Team threw in the ball and scampered across the gym. Emily took a pass and with one hand launched the ball over her head in a graceful arc, putting two more points on the board. As she celebrated, her eyes looked toward Nikki and for just a moment, she stopped. Her face was red from exertion, her expression odd. She snapped out of it and turned to guard McKenzie, the yellow player who had just bounced the ball off her foot.

Nikki braced herself in case the ball should come to her. It did. Banging off the end of her left index finger, the pain shot up her arm. The ball bounced to Gumball, who twisted and shot. Another air ball.

"I think that was closer," Gumball said.

Nikki held her swelling hand. "I think I have to stop."

The ref blew the whistle and approached. "That looks like it needs some ice. You go on to the nurse."

Gumball yelled toward the bench, "Come on, Asa! It's not the size of the body, it's the size of the heart."

Nikki whispered, "I bet his heart isn't very big."

"His bravery, dumbass. Go get your hand looked at."

The throbbing increased with each step as Nikki plodded to the medical room.

Chapter Eighteen

Pulling open the door with her good hand, Nikki choked on the cloud of antiseptics and pine cleaner.

The person at the desk looked up. "Sorry, we just had a puker, heat got to them. Have a seat. Are you left-handed?"

Nikki nodded.

"Then it looks like I should fill out the form for you. What happened?"

Nikki eased into the metal folding chair. "Um, well, it's probably nothing. I tripped, at basketball. I mean, fell. Doesn't matter, my hand is swollen."

Stephanie appeared from the next room. "Nice color already. Thankfully, we have a local doctor this year willing to see our patients if they don't need an ambulance, and he has an x-ray at the clinic. I'll just start you with some ice and then give him a call. I can drive you there, and then we'll get you patched up."

Nikki followed her to the camp transport van. She opened the door and Nikki climbed in while holding her arm close to her body.

Stephanie adjusted her phone and music began to play from the van speakers. She stomped on the brakes as a squirrel ran in front of the van.

"Shit," Nikki mumbled, clutching her wrist.

With the road clear, Stephanie eased the van forward. At a small strip mall, she turned in by the end building. "I'll sign you in."

They entered the lobby and Nikki took a seat near a fish tank. A striped fish picked at the gravel, and several yellow fish darted around coral. A faint scent of salt water was overpowered by the air freshener plugged into the wall.

A slender man in black scrubs called her name. "Nikki, follow me please. I'm Joel, I'll be taking a few pictures to make sure you haven't broken anything."

His black hair was short, except one lock that fell across his forehead. Shockingly blue eyes scanned over her arm. "Just have a seat and I'll adjust this thing so we can get you back to the fun. Is this your first year at Camp Iris?"

"Yes."

"That's where I met the doc, and we've been together ever since." He touched her arm. "I'm sorry if this hurts."

Nikki tried to keep still as he gently adjusted her wrist under the lighted crosshatches from the machine.

"Just there. Perfect. I'll be right back."

She watched him scurry to the next room. The machine made a humming noise and then he reappeared.

"One more. This one might smart a little."

Nikki winced as he rotated her arm. "Yikes." What if it was broken and she'd spend the rest of the time at camp with a cast? No more swimming, but maybe that was a plus. No more lake monsters.

"I'm sorry, honey. It'll take just a hot minute."

Nikki closed her eyes and took a deep breath, slowly blowing it out. The humming started, and she opened her eyes just as he walked toward her.

"Alrighty, you can follow me to wait for the doctor."

"You can't tell me anything?"

"We won't have to amputate." His laugh was more of a giggle. "I'm kidding, of course."

She forced a smile. "Of course." It sounded to her like it was broken.

The doctor stuck his head out from a doorway. "Just come on down. You're the next contestant on *The Price Is Right*."

Nikki groaned. In the tiny room, she sat on the examination table, the paper crackling as she wiggled.

The doctor tipped his head back as he read the screen. "The Camp Iris Color Wars are getting rough this year. So, tell me what happened."

"I fell. In the gym."

"Looks like the floor won. I am happy to report that you didn't break anything, but I would like to keep it immobilized a week or two, at least until some of the swelling goes down."

"I don't have to go home?"

"Only if you want to." Joel appeared with a package and opened the box. "This should fit, but you can adjust it here if you need to."

The stiff plastic straps hurt a bit as he fastened them.

Nikki asked, "At least a week?"

"I'd say so. It's up to you. You can take it off to shower, and at night, unless you box in your sleep."

"Not that I know of." Nikki stood. "Thanks."

The doctor patted her shoulder. "I hope to only see you again at the final talent Showcase. We go every year."

Joel waved. "Have a good afternoon."

After the short ride back to camp, Stephanie dropped her off near the cafeteria. "You don't need to come into the clinic. You might be able to get something before meal service is over."

Nikki scanned the dining room but couldn't find Gumball. Not willing to try a tray, she grabbed an apple and then began to look for a seat in the noisy room filled with teenagers.

A voice behind her called, "Nikki, are you all right?"

Miranda wore her usual tank top with coverall shorts, but the clothes were covered with paint splashes.

"What happened to you?"

"Some idiot from the Blue Team ran through flicking everyone. Mr. Novak is dealing with that. How's your arm? Is it broken?"

"No, just banged up a bit. It'll be fine in a day or two."

"I'm sorry you got hurt. Let me know if I need to reschedule some of your events. I'm guessing frisbee might be out."

Nikki nodded. "Maybe something safe like crossword puzzles?"

Miranda frowned. "Why don't we have that? I'm going to suggest it. We do have a puzzle challenge you do blindfolded. Can you wiggle your fingers at all?"

"Sure, when is it?"

Miranda tapped on her phone. "Tomorrow at three. Want me to get you a tray? The spaghetti is pretty good."

"No, thanks. I'm more tired than I thought. I might just head back to the cabin for some rest."

"I'm sure staying up half the night pranking the camp takes its toll," Miranda deadpanned.

"I'm sure I have no idea what you're talking about." Nikki shrugged. "I need to go test the program one more time for tonight. See you at the team meeting before dinner."

Miranda winked. "Yeah, see you."

As Nikki reached the door, Emily approached. "You okay?"

Nikki nodded and held up her wrist and sang, "I fought the floor and the floor won."

Emily whispered, "Want me to get you some ice cream?"

"Pardon?"

"You know, like from our little expedition."

"Oh, right. Ice cream." Nikki tried to smile. "No, I'm good. See ya."

"Yeah." Emily held the door and then hurried the other direction.

Nikki wandered to the cabin. Camp Iris made everyone act weird.

Gumball walked up and joined her stride for stride. "I missed you at lunch. Sadly, we suffered a loss, but the point spread doesn't matter. How's your wrist? Can you still do stuff?"

"Juggling is out, but otherwise, I can do what I want."

"Good. I need a sentry."

Gumball didn't add any more and Nikki was afraid to ask.

❧ ❧ ❧ ❧

Nikki and Gumball waited in the cabin while their roommates disappeared to their afternoon sessions. They snuck to the main building on the lookout for other campers who might wonder what they were doing. They hid when a group from their own Yellow

Team passed on the way to the next team challenge. Inside the cool air of the lobby, Gumball turned left and led the way to the computer lab. At the doorway, she held up a hand to indicate Nikki should stand guard. Gumball moved the gym bag off her shoulder and stepped into the computer lab. As the minutes dragged past, Nikki wondered what she would do if someone approached. That hadn't really been addressed. Should she just say hello super loud? Gumball might spend hours preparing these little pranks, but she left out some important details.

Thankfully, no one came down the hall.

Gumball opened the door. "Come take a quick peek and then let's get out of here."

Nikki surveyed the room. Several of the keyboards were growing some kind of green grass or something. "How did you—"

"Not now. Come on, but walk regular." Gumball tugged Nikki's arm.

Nikki couldn't think of anything to talk about that sounded camp related.

Gumball asked, "Is everything ready for the movie intro tonight?"

"I think so. The app works great, and Hunter set up the group text. McKenzie and Daniel were doing the cupcakes. Miranda has the rest of them decorating the cafeteria."

"What does Miranda think we're doing?"

"Testing the program."

With her right hand, Nikki pushed open the doors. Outside, she could finally ask, "Alright, how did you get grass to grow that fast?"

Gumball laughed. "It's brilliant, even if I say so. I got some old keyboards at Goodwill. When we got to camp, I set them up under my bunk near the wall. I dumped Chia pet seeds into the keys, watered it, and waited a couple days. Ta-da…keyboard lawns!"

Nikki snorted. "I wish we could see the looks on their faces when the next group uses the lab."

Gumball waved her phone. "I'm sure someone will post pics."

"It's too bad you don't get credit."

"More importantly, I don't get the blame." Gumball turned toward the snack shack. "Want an ice cream or something?"

❧ ❧ ❧ ❧

In the shade of a table umbrella, Nikki and Gumball sipped their slushies as they watched water Quadball. It may have been cooler in the water, but the splashing of noodles smacking wiffle balls was chaotic. It was impossible to determine who might be swimming toward victory, Team Yellow or Team Green.

"Daniel has an impressive wingspan," Nikki said. "How do you tell who's winning?"

"I have no idea. I just saw Nyssa toss a bag of rubber ducks in the pool. Maybe that's a new element."

"Don't know, don't really care." Nikki picked up her drink, the berry flavor a poor substitute for lime, which was more refreshing. "I'm more of a Star Trek fan."

"That explains your reluctance to do the lightsaber class."

"Hmm?"

"*Star Trek not Star Wars.*"

Nikki smiled. Gumball was an even bigger nerd than she was. "And you prefer?"

"*Dr. Who* of course, but my dad watched *Star Trek: The Next Generation* constantly. Mom made the mistake of getting a DVD set for him. She mentioned it every time the show theme started in the den."

Nikki tried to imagine the time when her parents got along but couldn't really think of anything. They were planets orbiting the same sun, occasionally sharing similar trajectories with little in common.

"So, which?"

Nikki focused on Gumball. "Which what?"

"Never mind. Look, Daniel just got beaned by two noodles at once."

Nikki glanced over. "Rough game, Quadball."

They both smiled.

⁂

That night during dinner, the Yellow Team combined their color event with the Eighties Night party theme. What would be better than a reference to a Marvel movie? What would be better than that reference going back to a movie from 1983?

Nikki cued up the sound board and waited for the signal. Gumball stretched the screen at the bottom corner and secured the fastener to the pole. She gave a thumbs-up, and Daniel hit the power button on the electric control box. The screen flashed the words and a robotic voice asked, "Shall we play a game?"

Nikki slid up the buttons and each speaker echoed, "Love to. How about Global Thermonuclear War?"

Tic-tac-toe boards materialized on everyone's Snapchat. Mr. Novak appeared at the front of the room, accepting a microphone from Gumball.

"Please join me in congratulating the Yellow Team on a wonderful coordinated display. I award your team the full two hundred points for theme and creativity. For those of you too young to know, which is probably everyone here but me, these lines quoted by Black Widow in the movie *Captain America: The Winter Soldier* are originally from the 1983 movie WarGames, which will be showing tonight at eight p.m. Flavored popcorn and soft drinks will be provided and it's a theme party. Let's go retro—Eighties Night, people."

Miranda shouted, "I have hashtag beads for everyone."

The campers rushed her.

Gumball grabbed Nikki's arm as they hurried back to the cabin. "I've got an MTV T-shirt if you need one."

"Nah, my mom gave me her old Poison shirt."

"I'm not sure if I'm impressed or distressed."

They both sang, "Every rose has its thorn."

Chapter Nineteen
July 28

Thomas, the leader of the Orange Team, approached the microphone. "Tonight will be the Eyes to the Skies search for constellations. Please make sure you've updated the app on your phone, and trust me, make sure you set the coordinates or you'll be looking for constellations in the southern hemisphere. Bring a towel or blanket to lay on and remember bug spray."

Mr. Novak appeared beside him. "I know you're all excited for our special off-campus activities day. You represent Camp Iris while on these field trips, so put on your best behavior. The hikers will be in bus number one for the trip to the waterfall. The horseback riders and the four-wheelers all will take bus two. For those remaining on campus, the frisbee golf will start at ten at the first hole near the pool. I have arranged a Pokémon event for our campus, so make sure your app is up to date. This evening there will be a bonfire near the lake including a sing-along led by the Blue Team."

Outside the auditorium, Gumball stood at the bus. "Are you sure you don't want to come? I'll switch to the hike too."

"Nah, thanks. I'll be fine." Nikki held up her arm. "I might do the Pokémon or something."

Gumball whispered, "I'll miss you."

Nikki smiled, but she doubted it. The minute

the four-wheelers started, there would be no thoughts in Gumball's mind but speed. Miranda said she'd get a refund for the cost, but at the moment, it was little consolation. She did suggest Nikki could go into the computer room to meet Nyssa for online gaming. There was better Wi-Fi in the building, and Nikki hoped a power game of D and D would take her mind off the fun she was missing off campus.

Nikki seemed the only one in the building as she approached the lab. It wasn't quite as exciting as the lab prank with Gumball. Inside the room, she spotted all the lawn keyboards together on a back table. Someone added a stick and labeled it Groot.

Nyssa was clicking away on a keyboard. She adjusted the camera. "Hey everybody, I have an extra player today. I gave her a player sheet. It's a surprise for the rest of you."

Nikki sat down next to Nyssa and accepted the paper.

**

The buses hadn't yet returned when the game was over. Nikki sat on the bench under the pine tree, a woodpecker knocking to find a snack. She took out her phone. Tapping the screen with two fingers, Nikki managed a short message to Georgi.

Sprained hand at basketball.
Since when?
Yesterday. I fell.
R u ok?
Hurts
Sounds like it, how's haircut girl?
I do like her
cool
Ttyl

※ ※ ※ ※

"Then we went across this creek, and if you stopped and then hit the throttle hard, water went like twenty feet in the air. It was so sick." Gumball carried Nikki's tray to the table at dinner.

"Nyssa let me play with her regular adventure. I got to play a dragon."

"I'm glad you had a good time today, but I don't know how that was more fun than four-wheelers."

Nikki winced. She had put up a good front, but Gumball was missing it. She tried to eat the tofu taco with one hand, most of the ingredients spilling out of the shell onto the plate. She picked up a fork and said, "I might skip the bonfire. My arm is pretty sore."

"Come on, it'll be fun."

"Fun like a flu shot?" Nikki shoved the food in her mouth.

"Ha ha." Gumball sang, "There's a sing-along."

"Humph."

"Come on, Nikki. I haven't hardly seen you all day."

The lure of time with Gumball was strong and Nikki relented. As they rounded the pavilion, Gumball pointed.

"I wonder what they're up to."

A group of campers clustered around an object, all bent over staring at the ground.

Nikki shrugged. They joined the group and peered at the giant footprints. Three to be exact.

Daniel said, "It's impossible to be a Bigfoot. There is no Bigfoot. Besides, why are there only three?"

Asa held his phone up to take a picture. "Because they walked on the gravel the rest of the way."

Gumball smiled. "It's a prank, dude. Just go to the bonfire."

Asa folded his arms in front of his chest. "Just because you can't see it doesn't mean it's not real."

Nikki felt bad for him. She said, "Right, like gravity."

Asa smiled.

They settled into the benches around the enormous pile of wood. The scent of pine mixed with bug spray, and more than a few teens that needed a shower. The bonfire flickered yellow light against the trees around them, the heat from the flames hot on her chest and the cool night air on her back. Gumball pressed her leg against her thigh. Nikki felt her mouth go dry. She slowly shifted her right hand over Gumball's left hand. Gumball linked her fingers to Nikki's. It was a perfect night, even if her wrist hurt.

Chapter Twenty
July 29

During a break in the morning build session, Gumball studied the point scores. "Nikki, look here. There's a notation of bonus points for team cooperation. Since we're going to be with the Blue Team, what could we do with them?"

"I can't even read music, so I'm not sure." Nikki pointed to Daniel. "All right, ideas."

Daniel answered, "Build a better synthesizer?"

McKenzie laughed. "Go simpler. Color each note and make a pattern from the music."

Gumball said, "I don't follow."

"Set a time element for each note, just like in the sheet music, but instead of hearing a pitch, a color would appear." McKenzie scratched her head. "I don't know what we'd do about chords."

Nikki said, "Couldn't there be more than one color on the screen at a time?"

"Blended?" Daniel asked.

Nikki shook her head. "No, that would be just other colors. Like a separate square for each."

"Great," McKenzie said. "That would work."

After several hours of programming, Gumball proclaimed the first demo ready to run. "Let's find the Blue Team and see what they think."

At the far side of the building, they stopped at the designated room and knocked.

Thomas answered the door. "No one but Blue

Team allowed."

"We made an app we want you to try," Nikki said.

"Give me a minute."

They heard scrapping of chairs and tables against the floor, then the door flew open. Thomas waved an arm. "Greetings, Yellow Team. Entrez-vous."

In the Blue Team music room, they huddled around the iPad and watched as color bubbles popped on the screen in time with the music, bursting into a kaleidoscope with the chords.

"This is just a start," Gumball said.

Thomas cheered. "This is already pretty cool."

Tony, now sporting a blue mohawk, grinned. "Pretty cool? It's sickening. Wait until I use it to teach kids to read music with color to support the concept, especially for those who have different learning styles or challenges with hearing. Can I get a copy of this?"

Gumball shrugged. "Sure, but only if you turn it into shareware later. Use the profits for the band instrument fund or something."

"You guys are awesome." Thomas gave them all high fives. "Just for that, I'm giving you beads with a music note on it."

"Great," Gumball said, her voice dripping with sarcasm Thomas seemed to miss or ignore.

McKenzie reached for Nikki's name tag. "Can I help you put the bead on?"

Nikki nodded and Gumball pouted.

**

A few hours later, Nikki sat in the gaming room with her sore arm resting on the table. Gumball, Daniel, Asa, and Elliot were all present.

Nyssa handed out checkered bandannas. "Your group sits blindfolded at this round table. One person sits out without a blindfold with his or her back to the group. They may not turn around to look at the group."

She scattered the puzzle pieces across the table, the wooden shapes clicking against the Formica. "The group must try to assemble the puzzle. The person who can see will have a picture of the image and can give directions to the group to help, but they may not look at the progress of the work."

Gumball said, "I don't like being restrained, so I'll give directions."

Daniel snickered. "That's a story I need to hear."

Nikki slid the fabric across her flushing face, unable to grab both ends to tie the blindfold.

"Nikki, let me help you," Elliot said.

"Thanks." His long fingers quickly made a knot.

"Elliot, you smell really good."

"Thanks, now let's do this thing."

Nyssa said, "Alright, get ready, the timer starts with the first directions you receive."

"Alright, Gumball, what shall we do first?" Daniel asked.

"Everyone reach out and take one of the pieces and try to figure out the general shape." Gumball paused. "Now, if you have a round one, move it toward the upper right corner of the board."

It seemed to take them forever before they could take off the blindfolds and survey their handiwork. It was a simple farm scene with only ten pieces.

Nyssa said, "You're the first team to complete it, if you can believe it."

They slapped high fives, except with Nikki.

At dinner, the Green Team had talked the cooks into dyeing the food. They had green beans, peas, and green mashed potatoes. The green cake left everyone's teeth colored. Skipping the evening skit competition, no doubt won by the Green Team's actors, Nikki went to sleep early. She barely started to dream when she got a text.

Nikki forced her eyes open. She tapped the phone to stop the vibration. It was from Gumball. Whatever this prank was, it better be fast because she was exhausted. She wrestled from the bedding and stuck her feet into tennis shoes without socks. Across the dark room, she could barely make out the form of her cohort, a backpack hanging over one shoulder. Nikki followed her out, and Gumball eased the door closed.

The insect chorus sang to them as they crossed the campus. At the last cabin, they slowed their steps. Gumball held up a hand for a moment. Nikki didn't hear anything. After she was certain no one was around, Nikki nodded. Gumball tugged at the handle, holding the door until they were both inside. She put both hands against the wood and slowed the pull of the closer. The gentle click assured no one would awaken.

Each footstep was slow and deliberate until they reached the bathrooms. Inside the first stall, Gumball pressed her lips together as she handed Nikki the box of glow sticks.

Briefly, their fingers touched, and Nikki shivered. She smiled at Gumball, who hadn't seemed to have had the same reaction. It was stupid to think someone that cool would like her.

Gumball whispered, "Wait. I forgot the gloves." She pulled them out of a pocket and held one up for Nikki to wiggle her hand into. She looked at the braced wrist. "Just don't get anything on that hand."

Nikki sighed and ripped at the packet, now more challenging with one hand in a rubber glove, and handed the glow stick to Gumball.

Gumball crushed the end of the plastic tube with scissors, the green goo leaking around the blades. She tipped it over the bowl, and the water turned light green and glowed.

"So who's going to see this?" Nikki asked.

"We aren't done."

"I assumed." Nikki tugged at the wrapper and opened another glow stick. "Here. Six more left."

Gumball finished the last toilet and tucked the messy tubes into a plastic bag. She flipped her gloves inside out and dropped them in the same bag. "Hand me yours."

Nikki held up her arm.

"Sorry, I forgot." Gumball pulled off the one glove and added it to the trash bag before tying it closed.

Nikki squinted and then whispered, "Shouldn't we do the rest of the bathrooms?"

"I thought about it, but this way we won't get caught." Gumball pushed the trash into the bin. "Let's go."

It took every glow stick to complete the phantom toilet effect and the room glowed with an eerie green. Nikki did as instructed and followed Gumball.

Gumball stopped in the hallway just at the door. She fished in her backpack and pulled out a red box. She tipped the box and out slid an old-fashioned alarm clock with bells on the top. She adjusted the dials.

"Slide the lever on the back, set it down, and don't run."

Nikki awkwardly did as instructed while Gumball slowly opened the door and held it for her. Outside they circled around under the windows. Nikki jumped as the shrill noise pierced the quiet air. She followed Gumball between the bushes and the wall as phone lights began to pop on. At the corner they turned and went along the tree line to the other building.

Gumball said, "I wish we could see the looks on their faces when they hit the johns."

"Maybe they won't even go in there until the morning."

"Someone will. I hope they take a picture."

"I guess we will hear about it either way."

Gumball snickered. "I'm counting on it."

Chapter Twenty-One
July 30

Gumball and Nikki wandered through the cafeteria line, each selecting fruits and cereal boxes. Behind them a loud voice said, "And then when I went to take a leak, I thought we'd had an alien invasion. I about wet myself. It was pretty funny though."

Gumball covered her laugh. She nudged Nikki. "Come on, we have to eat fast. Miranda is holding a Yellow Team poker practice in the command center."

Twenty minutes later, Nikki, Gumball, and Hunter sat on a couch and watched as Miranda shuffled, the cards fluttering from each hand into a neat pile. She then placed two cards face up in front of each of them, five cards face up between them all, and set down the remaining stack.

"You normally keep the two cards I put in front of you secret—they're called 'hole cards'—but for this first round we'll play so that everyone can see. All players can use their hole cards plus the cards in the middle to make the best five-card hand they can. Whoever makes the best hand at the table wins." Miranda adjusted a card. "The thing about learning to play poker is that you should fold more than not. Unless you think that your hand can win, of course."

Nikki studied the cards. Her first hand was a big loser.

"Now, let's look at each person's cards and

decide what they might play," Miranda said. "Check your game sheet, which you can use at the tournament. I checked the rules."

They studied the cards. Gumball said, "I have three of a kind."

"A pair," Nikki said.

Hunter grinned. "A full house."

"Yes, and I have a straight. Who wins?" Miranda asked.

"A straight wins over a full house," Nikki said.

"Only if it's one suit—a straight flush—and mine is mixed. Hunter would win. Let's try it again." Miranda dealt each person two cards facing down and then laid five face up on the table.

Gumball tipped her cards up and then covered them. "How do we do betting?"

"Let's not get ahead of ourselves. But basically, there's a fixed amount for every game to start, and players take turns with a larger forced bet. We use chips, of course. We all start with a thousand dollars' worth."

"What about bluffing?" Hunter asked as they pushed up their glasses.

Miranda looked at Gumball and cleared her throat. "Some of you are better liars than others, so that skill might transfer to poker. It's more important to understand the scoring to start."

For the next two hours, Nikki lost hand after hand.

Gumball was still enthusiastic. "Now that you know every way to lose, we're going to crush them. Come on, I want to touch up my hair."

Gumball stood at the mirror, the clippers buzzing as she edged around her ear. Nikki watched as the hair dropped onto the towel.

"I was thinking," Gumball said. "There's this chick here from my high school. Tracy totally drives me nuts. She's in some dance club and talks about it nonstop. She's on the Red Team. Her and Emily aren't in the same cabin, but they should at least know each other. Maybe we should hook them up?"

"I'm pretty sure she still hates me."

"She doesn't."

"Fine. Strongly dislikes."

"I could go with mildly."

"Argh. You know what I mean. Why would I get her a girlfriend?"

"Think about it. They both suck as human beings. If they date each other, it will protect two good people from a bad relationship."

Nikki smiled. "I like where you're going with this. How do we play Cupid?"

"I was thinking we could get a box of cookies and leave them on the cabin porch with a note for the prettiest girl at camp. They could just fight it out. But maybe I should put Tracy's name on it."

"Attention from some mystery person won't drive them together."

"Maybe not, but I can hack in and send some texts to them from each other."

"What if they figure it out later?"

"Who cares? Just another little prank, right?"

At the pool, Gumball and Nikki sat in the front row with McKenzie and Hunter behind them in the bleachers. The synchronized swim competition was nearly over. Each team did their routine for a points system. Nikki wasn't quite sure how they judged it. They all looked pretty good to her, but they cheered loudest as their teammates—Miranda, Asa, Aaron, Daniel, and Jesse—walked out on the pool deck for their recognition.

Nyssa held up her hands and then announced the final points would be posted later in the afternoon. Gumball's phone chimed. "Time for me to go. I'm headed to the Trans Ally workshop. You want to go?"

Nikki shook her head. "I promised Asa and Daniel that I'd help decorate our wagon for the Color Parade tomorrow morning."

"Seems biased everyone starts with a red wagon, don't you think?"

Nikki smiled. "Ours will be a tie-dye when we're done. We're adding music and two robots waving."

"Jesse is helping?"

"Yeah, they have a whole soundtrack already."

Gumball said, "I've got some extra speakers you can use if you need them."

Nikki waved as she left. "Thanks."

Chapter Twenty-Two
July 31

Nikki yawned as they sat at the beach near the canoes. "Why are we doing this before breakfast?"

Gumball said, "To help in case the little kids fall out and get scared."

"What if I fall out and get scared?"

"I'll save you."

Nikki rubbed at her wrist, wondering if she shouldn't have worn the brace. No. She didn't want lake water and seaweed in it.

Gumball stood up and said, "Change of plans. You stay at the beach. I'll see you for dinner."

Nikki watched her follow the path to campus.

A lifeguard said, "Thank you for volunteering. We have several water events over the next few weeks, and sometimes a civilian is closer to a victim than the lifeguard. You already know to throw a life ring if you're on the ground. We will practice some techniques in case you are already on the water." He walked to a canoe and rocked it with his foot. "Some of the little kids, or even bigger kids, are from the city and have never swum in a lake. They freak out if the boat tips over, and we want to work on how to keep them calm. Get a partner and paddle a canoe just to the middle of the swim area."

As Nikki reached a canoe, a familiar voice echoed behind her.

"Now for sure they'll drown." Emily had her hands on her hips and a frown on her face, but she winked.

"I can swim."

Emily pointed to her eye. "But you can't stop."

"Shut up. Just get in the boat." Nikki craned her neck to see what the next directions would be. At that moment, she realized she could have slept in, but now, here she was floating in the lagoon with Emily. Gumball was going to hear about this.

Over the bullhorn, the instructor said, "Now, just flip the canoe and stay underneath. You need to practice keeping someone calm."

Nikki's one hand clenched the paddle as Emily leaned the boat precariously close to flooding. The shock of the cold water made her jump, and before she could remember to drop the paddle, she heard Emily.

"Stand up."

"What?"

"There's air trapped in the canoe. Just stand up and open your eyes."

Nikki poked her feet downward and to her amazement she could stand. Once her head was clear of the water, she took a deep breath. "What do I do with the paddle?"

"Ride it back to shore."

"What?"

"I'm kidding. Stick it in the boat. When we flip the canoe, it will float even full of water."

"Really?"

"Yes. Really."

Nikki's teeth started to chatter. "How long do we stay under here?"

"I don't think he said."

Nikki frantically turned her head from side to side. "How long can we be here? We'll suffocate."

Emily lifted the edge of the boat and air whooshed in. "No, you won't. You're a good actress, I really think you're scared."

Nikki felt the panic tighten her throat. She gasped for air.

Emily softly said, "It's alright. Just look around. The light reflects under the boat. Take a slow, deep breath."

Never in a million years did Nikki think that Emily Morgan would actually help her from freaking out in the lake. Maybe she was just practicing, too.

Emily said, "That's it. One more big breath."

Nikki tried to breathe through her nose but couldn't. She gulped. "How much longer do you think?"

"We should be close to done. Put the paddle through the seat."

Nikki's fingers cramped on the handle. She willed herself to let go.

"There you go. Duck for a minute. Then grab the side."

Sunlight blinded her and the upright canoe banged into her shoulder. She pushed the oar toward the floor and clutched the side.

Emily said, "I sure hope we don't ever have to do this. Some of those younger campers are pretty small. You could lose track of them easy."

Nikki wasn't sure if she was kidding or not. "Some of those kids swim like Olympians."

The bullhorn squealed. "Okay, that's about it. Bring the boats back to shore."

"You want to climb back in or just swim it to

shore?"

Nikki glanced to the shore and realized she was still standing. She envisioned the spectacle of getting back into the canoe. "Let's just walk it in."

"Whatever you say." Emily guided the boat to point to shore.

"Thanks."

Emily looked confused for a second and then nodded. "No problem. You'd do the same for me."

Nikki hoped that was true.

❧❧❧❧

In the camp commons, Miranda stood behind Gumball and Nikki as they studied the score chart.

Gumball said, "My plan is working perfectly."

"Perfectly?" Miranda said. "We're in fourth place. Even with our second place in the Color Parade. No one would expect us to win."

"Exactly. We're entering the cerebral contest portion. They won't know what hit them."

Miranda raised an eyebrow. "I'm not sure of this approach."

"Trust me, doubting Miranda. We will win it all. Fame and eternal glory."

"I have a staff meeting. You guys go get to work on the robots. It might be our only chance."

They passed a table in the lobby with boxes of donuts. Gumball flipped open the lid revealing a vegetable tray. Miranda burst out laughing. "Good one. Bye."

Nikki watched Miranda leave and took a carrot stick.

Daniel whispered, "I guess there are more

pranksters this year."

Gumball closed the lid. "Ha ha. What a stupid trick. It's not really that funny. At least it wasn't donuts filled with toothpaste, I suppose."

"There is funny and then there is downright mean." Asa crossed his arms.

"It's too bad they don't give points for epic pranks," Gumball mused.

"Don't you even think about it," Daniel said. "You're going to lose us points when you get caught."

Gumball shrugged. "If, not when."

"You hope." Nikki took a celery stick. "Let's get to work."

⁂

After meticulously programming the movements of each individual robot, the team stood watching the machines in the middle of the room. Gumball hunched over the keyboard, muttering a steady stream of obscenities.

The little dancers began to move. Arranged in a row, they all twirled in a circle, then formed a line and began to swing their arms.

Daniel held up a hand. "Stop. Right there, the arms aren't going up fast enough."

"Or far enough. Are they binding?" Nikki studied the structure. "Seems clear."

Gumball said, "It's the program. Hang on, I've got to fix it. Anything else need tweaking? I just added another movement."

McKenzie started the music again. "Ten different operations not enough?"

"Maximum points for creativity. I want to amaze

people, not daze them to sleep."

The song started again, and they scrutinized the movements.

Randomly, different robots seemed to freeze and then restart. Soon the entire group was out of sync.

Daniel shot a glare at Gumball.

Gumball put a piece of bubble gum in her mouth. "You want to take over, Einstein?"

"No, it's just, it must be a simple mistake. Let me see."

"Touch one key and I'm done," Gumball said. "I'm not kidding."

Nikki held up her hands. "Okay, folks. It's been a long afternoon. Let's take a look tomorrow with fresh eyes."

❧❧❧❧

In line for dinner, Emily came up behind Nikki and Gumball. "Still hungry even after all those donuts?"

Gumball winked. "I don't know what you mean. We aren't supposed to pull pranks."

Emily leaned closer. "We aren't supposed to get caught doing pranks."

They laughed and then Emily seemed to notice Nikki. "Hi."

"Hi yourself."

"You two a thing?" Emily asked.

Gumball shrugged. "You missed your chance. You seeing someone?"

Emily flushed. "Too busy with sports."

Gumball jabbed her arm. "Don't let all the good ones get away."

Emily looked as if she wanted to say something but didn't. She took her tray. "See you, Gumball."

Chapter Twenty-Three
August 1

Mr. Novak wore shorts and a tank top when he walked to the podium. "Welcome to August. It's hard to believe we're halfway through our third week of camp. Is everyone having a good time?"

The audience cheered and clapped.

"Y'all are sounding a little tired. I may have to pass out sports drinks before the canoe races. Everyone report to the beach. It's double elimination in head-to-head matches. At least four team members in each canoe, five are allowed."

On the way out of the auditorium, Nikki tapped Daniel. "Why would you want more?"

"Well, if they're light enough but can paddle well, it helps. Otherwise, it's dead weight." He flexed his arm. "I'm not sure who else can actually canoe on our team."

Gumball cleared her throat. "I'm excellent at canoeing, and so is Nikki."

Nikki protested, "I am not that good, honest."

Daniel held up a hand. "Look around at our team. We need the tallest and the littlest." He started tapping on his phone.

Miranda grabbed his arm. "If you ask anyone their weight…"

"Fine." He shoved his phone in his pocket.

On the way to dinner, Nikki noticed the orange flyers all over camp, on bunks, stapled to bulletin boards, and a few on the tables in the cafeteria. The image of a porcupine in the top corner identified the team responsible.

Taped to the tables was a manifesto.

POLITICS is not important. Unless you care about civil rights, clean water, clean air, fair taxes. Please follow us on Snapchat for posts related to immediate action. Together we can make a difference. There are a hundred of us, plus all of our friends. Share the link only with other like-minded individuals. Immediate action: If you are eighteen, register to vote today.

Nikki scrolled over her screen and tapped the glass. "And done."

Miranda nodded. "Same, and I'm already registered to vote."

The din in the room quieted as fellow campers worked on their phones. In moments, Nikki's phone pinged with a welcome shot of a smiling baby porcupine eating a pumpkin. "Have you seen the video of the porcupine eating a pumpkin? He squeaks and it's darling."

Gumball sat down. "You don't have to call me darling, darling."

"Honestly? You know that song?" Miranda said.

"I am not only extremely smart, I'm culturally sensitive." Gumball laughed. "I'm kidding. My grandfather listens to that old country western stuff. Mostly to drive my grandma nuts, I think."

Nikki said, "And the question is, how do you know it, Miranda?"

"I can't share. It brings back too many painful

memories of car trips from my childhood. I'm glad we don't have a singing competition."

Jesse danced up to the table. "You might be surprised."

"Doubt it," Miranda said. "The sing-along is painful enough. Don't be late."

❧❧❧❧

Back in the cabin, only Nikki and Gumball were left as everyone else had already gone to the pavilion for the sing-along.

Gumball pulled a bottle of probiotics from her pocket. "Give me a hand."

Nikki held up her wrist brace. "Funny."

"No, just open these and dump out the contents. Be careful not to get them wet."

Nikki raised an eyebrow but knew Gumball had some nefarious purpose in mind. The capsules were not as easy to pull apart as she thought, and she'd smashed a few. "Sorry, I just can't quite get these."

"No biggie. We got plenty." Gumball took out some Kool-Aid packets. "You can buy powdered food color, but Kool-Aid is super cheap."

She tore a tiny corner off the first packet and poured it into half of a capsule and handed it to Nikki. "Can you get them back together?"

"I think so." Without spilling any, she managed to close the pills. "Why are we doing our own showers?"

"No one will think to look at anyone in our cabin, and it's pretty immature." Gumball had several colors of Kool-Aid, and soon they had dozens of capsules. "I'm not really sure how long they will last, but I wanted to try a variation of the shower prank. It should at least show color for a bit and be funny."

With pliers, Gumball twisted off the screen to the faucet, stuffed in a paper towel to make sure it was dry, then added a couple capsules. "Tonight, there should be a rainbow."

They ambled toward the pavilion, the music floating over the camp. The evening air was mystical until they were interrupted.

Miranda caught up with them. "I notice you're late. I hope no underwear is on the flagpole."

Nikki laughed. "That's pretty juvenile, don't you think."

Miranda squinted.

Gumball pulled some googly eyes from her pocket. "I guess we're busted."

Miranda put her hands on her hips. "Well, someone or someones have been really pulling the pranks, and Mr. Novak is concerned they may go too far and someone could get hurt."

"Like toilet paper in the trees? That would be awful," Nikki said.

"Or air horns on a chair." Gumball tapped her chin.

Miranda sighed. "Stop. I know it's you two. Just don't get caught. I want team champions, and you would cost us all our points."

"I'm pretty sure there are many culprits," Gumball said.

"So you admit it?"

"Admit what?" Gumball shrugged.

"I have to say the locker room prank was hilarious." Miranda laughed. "It took until the last volleyball game for someone to figure out there wasn't actually anyone in the stalls."

Nikki choked back laughter.

Gumball deadpanned, "We didn't sign up for volleyball."

"I know you're busy with the build, but if you could talk to Marcus on the Orange Team, I think you might be able to help him out."

"Oh?"

"He's got a cousin in Florida who's really upset about all the homophobia. I wondered if you might… you know."

"Cause some online mischief?"

"Exactly," Miranda said. "By the way, the Perseid meteor shower should start tonight. A bunch of us are headed out. It's late, though. You're used to that, I guess. Anyway, it should appear between two a.m. and dawn. I'd try the beach or the fields."

**

After midnight, Gumball and Nikki took a blanket and binoculars and strolled to the lakefront. In the dark air, a light breeze whispered through the trees, the scent of pine mixed with some scent Gumball was wearing.

Nikki wanted to grab her hand but was afraid.

Gumball said, "You never said if you have a girlfriend."

"I thought you did."

"Well, mostly friends that happen to be girls." She waved a hand over her body. "With all this, I try to keep the chicks from chasing me all camp. Therefore, I just say that."

Nikki considered this new information. "No. I don't have a girlfriend. I mean, before camp I really didn't say anything to anyone about liking girls. Women. It was my business, you know."

"Good. That you don't have a girlfriend. I got you something." Gumball pulled out a glow-in-the-dark bracelet. "I would have got champagne, but I'm seventeen, and you know, Dr. Pepper isn't much of a substitute."

Nikki accepted the gift and slid it on her wrist. "Thank you. It's beautiful."

Gumball reached over and took her hand. Nikki felt her pulse pounding in her ears. She knew Gumball would feel her sweaty palm.

"Is this okay?"

Nikki nodded. "Yes, but isn't it weird? Since we're friends?"

"No. Unless you'd rather date enemies."

Nikki laughed. "Since we're setting up Emily and Tracy, I guess I have to date friends."

Gumball stopped walking and faced her. "Good."

Ever so gently she touched her lips to Nikki's. Time stopped, sound disappeared, the night air stilled, and all that was left was the warmth on her mouth and the scent of Gumball. Nikki shivered, and then just like that, the kiss was over, and they were walking, holding hands. The crunch of their feet on the gravel as they neared the lake joined a chorus of frogs or bugs or something. Nikki wasn't sure and didn't care. She was holding Gumball's hand. She smiled in the dark.

Nikki stopped at the beach. "Is this good?"

Gumball spread out the blanket. She sat and patted the empty space next to her. "I won't bite."

"That's a disappointment." Nikki sat down, their legs touching together. She quaked in the warm air, excited and nervous. She reached over and touched Gumball's cheek.

Gumball pointed toward the sky. "Do you see the

planets? You should be able to find Mars and Saturn." She handed Nikki the binoculars.

Nikki frowned. Instead of cuddling or something, they really were going to look at the stars. She adjusted the focus and swept the sky. "Mars is the red dot. Yeah, I got it. Is Saturn that oval thing? I thought there were rings?"

"Sometimes you can see its moon Titan, but we really need a telescope. Maybe you can come to my house, and we can use my dad's."

"That would be great. Then I can spend the night."

"You'd have to stay on the pull-out couch. My parents know I'm queer and they won't let my brother or me have overnight guests in our rooms until we're eighteen."

"Well, that's rude."

"Their house."

"Can I call you Caitlyn sometimes?"

Gumball smiled. "You can call me anything you want, but I might not answer. Look."

She pointed. "We should be able to see Sagittarius. Okay, start at the horizon and look up."

"How far?"

"Maybe a third, before halfway for sure."

"It looks like a teapot."

"Well, it's Sagittarius. The meteor shower won't start for an hour."

"What should we do until then?" Nikki lay back on the blanket.

Gumball snuggled in and whispered, "I have a few ideas."

Chapter Twenty-Four
August 2

Miranda made the camp announcements. "Today's schedule includes poker, volleyball, and the finals for dance routine. Best of luck to everyone. Remember to hydrate. It's going to be a scorcher."

As Nikki and Gumball walked past the pool, there were already swimmers racing down the lanes.

Gumball snapped a bubble. "Maybe those people actually like to swim. Just to swim. So weird."

"So weird." They turned toward the pavilion. Clear of any other campers, Nikki said, "I left the cookies. What's next?"

"We set it up so the computer will send the texts in a couple hours."

"You're pretty romantic."

"Practice."

Nikki frowned.

Gumball laughed. "I'm kidding. My mom watches a lot of Hallmark movies. I mean, a LOT of them. I'll see you later."

"You're not going to watch the dance-off?"

"No, I've got a thing."

"A thing."

"It's a surprise."

Nikki scoffed. "Not an Emily-type surprise, or a prank?"

"No, I just can't tell you yet. I'll see you at the

robot build."

❧ ❧ ❧ ❧

When Nikki walked into the build lab, she found Gumball scribbling away on a sheet of paper. Across the table, a dozen pages stretched from one side to the other.

Gumball didn't look up. "Sometimes I like to get a visual on it all, and then I can see little variations."

Nikki thought she was nuts. The string of commands always looked like hieroglyphics whether on the screen or not. There was no mention of her mystery activity, just business as usual.

Nikki took out a screwdriver and began with the first robot, inspecting battery placement and the routes of the gears. "This one is backward. The little gear should be on the inside, or it won't move fast enough."

"Good find." Daniel set down a paper bag. "I'm sorry for getting impatient. I brought donuts to make up for it."

"I found it." Gumball scribbled and then stood. "We're a team. We win as a team."

Daniel shouted, "Halleloo!"

Asa came in. "You think we'll win."

Nikki shrugged. "Why not?"

**

The rain tapped against the windows as Nikki and Gumball snuck into the computer lab. They jumped as the thunder popped above the building.

Gumball said, "The pool races are over until the storm passes." She pulled out a chair. Once seated, Gumball typed on the keyboard as Nikki looked over her shoulder. "I already put in the code. All we need is the text contents. Here's what I have so far."

"*I'm so glad you are at camp, but I want to be more than friends.*"

"*Maybe the fantasy is better than reality, but I would love to see what would happen if we were together.*"

"*I never felt like this before. When you are in the room I am overwhelmed by my feelings. When I am just near you I feel happy.*"

"*I would love to be the one to make you laugh and smile every day.*"

"*No matter how hard I try to think about something else, my thoughts go back to you.*"

"That should be enough," Gumball said. "Let me set the timers." The rattling of the typing was barely louder than the rain.

Nikki looked at her phone. The message was from a random number she didn't have in her contacts. *Even when you are not around, I can't help but smile when I think of you. What would you wish for if you could make one wish?*

She looked at Gumball. "Did you send a message to me by mistake?"

"Shhh. I'm not done here." Gumball typed furiously.

A few dots scrolled then stopped. What if Gumball meant to send it, and Nikki just upset her? It was her first girlfriend, and Nikki was unsure of what to do. More dots, then they stopped.

Nikki typed furiously. *When I make a wish, the first person I think of is you.*

For several moments, nothing. Nikki's stomach sank. Then the dots started. *I thought I'd send a message to my girl too.*

She smacked the chair. "Dammit, Gumball. You gave me a heart attack."

Nikki grinned. Her girl. Camp Iris was awesome. When they exited the building, a rainbow appeared over the campus.

❧ ❧ ❧ ❧

Laughter and voices ricocheted around the cafeteria as Nikki carried her lunch tray to the table of students in orange. Hunter and Daniel followed closely behind her.

Over the din, she said, "Miranda told us about your challenge with the politician from Florida. We're here to help, if you don't mind."

"Yeah? I'm Jared, have a seat."

Marcus, their team leader, said, "We have an idea. Remember when that grandma in Iowa got everyone to sign up for tickets to Trump's rally, then everyone thought it was going to be a big crowd, and then they didn't go so it was almost empty? We could do that."

"Yeah, he was going to speak on Juneteenth. Pissed me off, too," Nikki said.

Hunter said, "They used TikTok to get out the message. I mean, you could use whatever social media you want, but you don't need real people."

"I don't follow." Marcus rubbed his ear.

"Well, we can create a program to generate email accounts, then automatically sign up with a macro. I mean, I can't, but Gumball can." Nikki waved down Gumball. "Hey, have a seat. We need someone with your particular skill set."

Gumball slid her tray down. "At your service."

"We're programming a little social backlash. The

dude who wants to fire teachers for saying gay.”

"Oh, I am so in. What do you have in mind?”

"Well, this politician is having an event, and we thought maybe we could tie up the free tickets like they did in Iowa.”

Hunter said, "We need bots.”

"You don't think Russians are the only ones with bots?” Nikki said.

"Bots?” Jared asked.

"Autonomous programs that collect and distribute data, but it's fallible if you know what to look for.” Gumball smiled.

"Like spam?”

"Right.” Gumball nodded.

Nikki said, "Let's head to the computer lab.”

Gumball starting doodling on the front whiteboard. "It would be easy to create a script to sign up for the tickets. We just need to use a free email account to sign up a whole bunch at one time. I'll write a script to create the accounts and then to respond to the verification messages from the email service.”

"What about the IP addresses?” Nikki asked.

"The what?” Marcus scrunched his eyebrows.

"IP identifies the individual computers,” Nikki said.

Hunter explained further. "The program creating the accounts would have to look like it's from different IP addresses or the bot program may look like a distributed denial-of-service attack. Once your accounts are set up, then the script can sign up for event tickets, again coming from different IP addresses.”

Gumball shrugged. "Most of these sites have humanity checkers, so we should hire a CAPTCHA/ humanity checker solver service to bypass the humanity checker security."

"You can also buy DDoS attacks cheap," Hunter said. "You'd be amazed how many students buy DDoS attacks to keep the parent portal down so their parents don't find out the student flunked a class."

Jared said, "What? You are kidding me."

Gumball nodded. "Or you could take the school down because exams are online."

Marcus grinned. "I have got to keep y'all on speed dial. I've got a credit card from my mom for emergencies. I'm sure she'd agree this is critical. Order whatever we need."

A few hours later, every computer in the lab softly whirred.

Jared smiled. "It's a thing of beauty. A little scary, but beautiful."

Mr. Novak shook an umbrella and cleared his throat. "I am not sure I want to know what you are getting up to, but in the spirit of team cooperation, I award thirty points to both Team Yellow and Team Orange. Carry on."

**

Nikki pushed open the door and stopped. The entire hallway was covered with small paper cups filled with, presumably, water.

"How are we going to get to the lab?" Asa asked.

Gumball swiped her foot and several cups tipped over. "I'll head for the janitor closet and get a mop and bucket."

"Wait!" Hunter held up their phone. "Let me get a shot of this."

Nikki laughed. "Who should we Photoshop into the picture setting this up?"

Miranda answered behind her. "Justin."

Gumball snickered. "Just knock a path to our room."

McKenzie touched Gumball's sleeve. "If you snap that gum one more time, I'm going to throat-punch you."

Gumball shrugged. "Kung fu Barbie need more sleep?" She blew a bubble and turned to the supply closet.

"Not now. No division in the ranks." Miranda unlocked the door, and the team sat around a table. "Everyone ready for our first run-through?"

Nikki waited. McKenzie and Jesse entered, followed by Daniel.

Aaron said, "We should send the pic out of us cleaning up the hallway."

Asa grinned. "Do I get to knock them over first?"

"As soon as Gumball gets here with the mop." Nikki gave Asa a fist bump. "Then you get a broom and dustpan to pick them up."

Hunter held up his phone. "Okay. I'm ready. Hit it."

Asa ran and slid into the cups, causing a splash followed by cups flying like bowling pins.

Hunter laughed. "This is epic."

Nikki held open the door. "How about we make our Showcase epic too?"

Gumball rode the mop like a child on a hobby horse, pulling the bucket behind her. "Be right back, compadres."

Nikki shook her head. It would take two miracles to succeed. Miranda would have to keep them from killing each other, and the robots would have to work perfectly.

May the odds be in our favor.

Chapter Twenty-Five
August 3

I heard the artists made the papier-mâché masks for the dancers for the finale." McKenzie put a lock of hair behind her ear.

Gumball said, "Won't matter. We're going to crush this archery challenge."

"Only because we're against the Orange Team?" Nikki asked.

"No idea who we are up against. But we have physics on our side." Hunter held their arms up like an archer releasing an arrow. "It's in my name. It's my destiny. It's—"

McKenzie pulled at his elbow. "Save some of it for the competition."

They went to the sign-in table where Lulabelle waited.

Nikki held up her braced wrist and asked, "I'm not asking for any allowances, I just was hoping you might have a suggestion for me to participate."

"Is it broken?"

"No. Just bruised it."

Lulabelle rubbed her ear. "You decide for yourself if you can do it or not. Take a few practice shots at the target. If it hurts too much, your team can use a substitute, or you'll have to scratch."

Nikki picked up a bow. "It's not cheating to use the brace?"

Lulabelle rolled her eyes. "People use wrist

guards to shoot a real bow. With these elementary school bows and arrows? I don't see how it would be much of a help or hindrance."

Hunter leaned toward Nikki's ear. "Just say fine, and we'll cover for you even if you don't shoot. You can watch and not get shot."

Nikki smiled. "Thanks, I'll go test it out."

"We start in fifteen minutes."

❧❧❧❧

Nikki's shirt clung to her body, her hair glued to her forehead. But she was uninjured, probably due in part to Emily's absence on the field. She caught herself. That was the old thinking. Positive changes need positive thinking. Be glad to have no new injuries.

"We did pretty well," Gumball said.

McKenzie huffed. "It was a tie. We are so bad we tied the Orange Team."

Miranda dabbed her shirt sleeve on her forehead. "But it's not a loss, either. The big events are coming up."

"Do you know what they are?"

"Yes," Miranda admitted. "I'm not allowed to say."

"What good is that?" Hunter asked.

"Trust me, it won't help if you do know." Miranda left the group to talk to the other team counselor.

McKenzie said, "I don't even want to imagine what we can't practice. Hammer throw? Jousting? On a bridge? Over a creek? With alligators?"

Chapter Twenty-Six
August 4

The schedule listed only "fun" on the calendar for this day. Curious campers straggled into the auditorium. The lights dimmed, and the sound of a waterfall drowned out the chatter. Sunshine Fanta arrived at the podium in a swimsuit with a fabulous flowered cover-up and a sun hat. "Good morning! It is a glorious day at Camp Iris."

The room darkened, and the video screen burst into a color drone feed with images of a floating aquapark. There were yellow, red, and blue obstacles to climb on and around, trampolines, slides, and water pads.

"As we speak, there is a crew at the lakefront inflating a water playground for our camp!"

A buzz of excitement went through the dark auditorium. Nikki glanced at Gumball and smiled. Asa was bouncing so hard he almost levitated.

"For today's fun day, if you have passed the swim test, you are welcome to put on your water socks and a life vest for a plethora of refreshing activities. I would remind you to wear sunscreen and consider a hat. There will be food trucks coming in for lunch and dinner today. If you have a special allergy diet, the cafeteria will have boxed meals ready for you. As usual, the lakefront will be closed to swimming in the evening, but you're welcome to use the beach area.

"We will have a karaoke contest in the auditorium

starting at eight this evening. Enjoy your day."

By the time they got changed and walked to the beach, most of the camp was in the lake. Giant blow-up floats strung together to form a massive maze of fun. An enormous square at the end of the dock bounced as people launched themselves from the platform, landed on the bright yellow blob, and were tossed in the air again before splashing in the water.

Nikki picked her way down the lawn to the dock. At a bench, she wiggled on her water socks. She selected a vest and the lifeguard checked the fit and that all clips were locked shut. She hung her badge on the board and joined the line. Gumball took a running start and whooped and jumped toward the float.

Nikki hesitated. She clutched the thick rope and jumped with less enthusiasm, the landing on the blow-up softer than she expected. She dropped into the water and the life vest popped her to the surface.

With a few dozen strokes, she reached the edge of the aquapark. The younger kids were like popcorn kernels popping inside the trampolines. The taller campers were climbing around the outside of a pyramid, bouncing as the kids leaped inside. At the tallest slide, several swimmers goaded each other into jumping into the water rather than sliding down.

Gumball was already in a bouncing competition with Emily. As Nikki pulled herself onto the floating pad, she heard someone from high on a twenty-foot slide scream, "A monster!"

Everyone peered in the water until a voice called, "On the shore. Look!"

Someone dressed in a ghillie suit raised his arms like a mummy in a movie, wandering the waterfront. Two counselors climbed the ladder to the dock and hurried to the beach. Before they could reach him, he sprinted to the locker room.

Evidently, he recognized this and decided to go down in a glorious fireball. He stopped, pulled off the hat and face mesh, and took a bow. Ryan. Team Red. Of course.

The swimmers called out, some cheering and some jeering. The counselors were laughing as they walked him toward the main building. The worst they could do was take points away.

Nikki climbed next to Gumball and Emily.

Gumball grinned at Emily. "Nice attempt. I'll give you credit for style, but it was lacking in execution."

Emily raised an eyebrow. "You could do better?"

"Challenge accepted." Gumball dove into the water.

Nikki shrugged. "I have no idea what you two are talking about." She dove after Gumball.

Chapter Twenty-Seven

August 5

Nikki woke to an announcement. "In life, most moments of glory pass by unrecorded. This sighting of the Lake Iris swamp monster is an exception. We present to you the scene of the monster at the lake yesterday afternoon."

Cell phones began to ping and vibrate as message alerts announced the incoming video. The short clip showed a close-up of the monster and then campers across the aquapark as they screamed and pointed. There was a second close-up. The final image was a shot of a sign reading "Nice prank, Yellow Team."

"Son of a bitch," Gumball said.

Miranda shrieked. "Yellow Team? There's no way. It was that Jolly Green Giant Ryan from the Red Team." She struggled to get dressed and left the cabin.

Nikki laughed. "The video is almost as good as the ghillie suit stunt itself."

Gumball whispered, "Just wait. I have something magnificent planned."

Nikki wondered what beat a camp-wide video.

On the way into the auditorium for morning notices, they peered up at the video screen. There was a montage of pictures of the swamp monster at various locations around camp, first at the tennis court, the strands of grass flying out as he hit the ball. At the volleyball court at the beach, he leaped to spike a ball.

Another shot was near the pool deck in a lawn chair with a fruit drink and garnish.

Mr. Novak appeared at the side of the stage. He was waving his arms as he spoke to several staff who then scattered. He strode to the podium and the screen went blank behind him.

"Good morning. I hope that you're all having a fabulous camp experience. Today we resume our regular schedule of activities. Justin asked that I remind you LARP costumes are discouraged for the lightsaber duels. I always say fashion before function, but evidently someone got tangled in their robes." He paused. "Where did Kylo Ren get his lightsaber? At the Darth Mall."

Several groans came from around the room.

"There are still some pranksters out there, and I remind you that our Showcase is but a week away and that all of your energies might be better focused on the success of that endeavor. Have a wonderful day."

※ ※ ※ ※

At lunch, Gumball slammed her hand down on the table, jostling the drink glasses. "I don't know how they did it. Dang. It was brilliant."

"I heard the staff is livid. They're worried the video will get out, go viral, and out a bunch of people."

"I suspect someone on our team helped them with both playing the video at the camp meeting and sending the feed to all the cell phones." She stared around the room at fellow Yellow Team tech students. "A traitor is in our mix."

Nikki scoffed. "I highly doubt it. Some of the smartest kids at our school are also athletes. I'm not sure about the dancers, though. I only know my stepsister, and she's not very academic."

"And you are?"

"Good point."

"Our grand final event will be talked about for years."

Miranda sat down. "What event?"

Nikki quickly said, "Our robots, of course."

Gumball nodded.

Marcus from the Blue Team walked past with a teammate. "If you say 'this one time at band camp' one more time, I'm going to strangle you."

Nikki couldn't hear the answer, but the expression was hostile.

Gumball winked. "Seems everyone is getting a little crabby."

"Not me," Nikki said.

"You think." Gumball blew her a kiss.

"I want a nap."

Miranda said, "Can't. We have the lightsaber competition."

"Great. That should really help my mood," Nikki mumbled.

❧❧❧❧

Nikki clutched the plastic handle and stared down at the floor.

Miranda touched her shoulder. "Look, it's not your fault you hurt your wrist. But this is a team event. We need six and the others are too small. You're going to have to at least go out there."

Nikki looked up as the Red Team marched across the stage in unison, chanting the Darth Vader theme song. It was not a good omen.

"What do I have to do?" Nikki regretted ditching the lightsaber class.

"Well, each of us fights individually, and then we get points based on the total wins. It's not winner takes all or anything."

Miranda handed her a fencing mask. "I put you in first, although I now realized it might have been better to let you watch."

Gumball said, "I'm not sure how much that would help."

Nikki shot her a look. She pulled on the mask. "Is that really necessary?"

"We wore masks with a foam arrow, remember?" Gumball waited beside her. "The force is with you."

Nikki stumbled to the mat. It was difficult to see the switch on the flashlight that lit up the saber. Before she could flick it on, the Red Team member smacked her in the side of the head. She was already off-balance and dropped to the floor.

The Red Team resumed the chanting. Nikki stood up and left the mat.

"Not off to a great start, are we?" Nikki undid the helmet.

"We're fine. Daniel is pretty good," Gumball answered. "Are you okay?"

"Oh yeah, I'm fine."

The next combatants, their Daniel and Ryan from the Red Team, put on their masks. He flicked on the plastic saber and stepped to the mat. The competitors danced back and forth like sword fighters until the last moment. Nikki watched in horror as the Red Team member charged Daniel and hit him under the chin. He dropped like a load of bricks. The referee raced to the mat.

Daniel stood up. "I'm fine. It's but a flesh wound."

Nikki said, "He must be okay if he's quoting Monty Python."

"I don't care," Miranda said. "I'm withdrawing our team on grounds of unfair play and risk of injury. I'm filing a protest."

Ryan strutted around the stage. "Two down, the rest too chicken to play."

"See, I told you," Gumball said. "They underestimate us."

"For good reason. Let's go."

As they hurried across campus, rain splashed off the sidewalk and thunder echoed across the camp.

The speaker crackled. "Due to possible rain this afternoon, motorcycle riding for beginners has been delayed until tomorrow."

"If this is possible rain," Gumball said, "I'm afraid what actual rain might look like."

Nikki wondered if they got to ride motorcycles or if it was more of a lecture. It would be more fun if they rode. "You heading to the build lab?"

"No, you go ahead. I have to check on something."

Nikki watched as Gumball's figure disappeared through the rain.

❧❧❧❧

At dinner, Nikki spotted Emily and Tracy eating together.

Gumball nudged her. "Looks like the plan worked."

When Emily and Tracy stood to leave, Nikki put down her fork. "Marcus from the Blue Team needs a favor."

"Since when do we help the Blue Team?"

"Just when it helps us." Nikki followed Emily and Tracy into the hallway. "Hey."

Emily stopped. "Yes?"

"I have something to say to you."

Emily pecked Tracy's cheek. "Go ahead. I'll be there in a minute."

Tracy nodded and left.

Emily set a hand on her hip. "I'm waiting."

Nikki looked around and then leaned in. "In strictest confidence."

"Okay."

"Marcus from the Blue Team has been trying to grow a condom garden."

"Is that some sort of code?"

Nikki shook her head. "He put the condoms over part of a toilet paper tube and wants to stick them in the dirt near the bushes so when the gardeners water, up come condom flowers."

Emily raised an eyebrow. "You're telling me this why?"

"Well, just in case you knew anyone that had more knowledge of the ratio of baking soda to, say cola, to launch them up." Nikki raised her eyebrows. "Not you personally, of course, but you may know some prankster with that skill base."

"Gumball wasn't up to it? Figures."

Nikki shrugged. "She doesn't see the value in diversifying the potential list of guilty parties. So to speak."

"Ah. Well, the rain is a problem, but I know a guy." Emily winked.

"Oh, and is that girl someone special?"

"Tracy? Maybe."

"She has beautiful eyes."

"She does, doesn't she? Well, I should go catch up with her. I'll make sure Marcus gets some help."

"Thanks." Nikki grinned and went back to the cafeteria.

❧ ❧ ❧ ❧

"Thank goodness the rain stopped." Mr. Novak spoke into a bullhorn as he wandered in front of the huge pile of wood. "I know all the staff join in congratulating you on a fantastic session at Camp Iris. The next two days will finish up team events in the color tournament with the escape room and the mega team phenomenon of the zombie apocalypse.

"I am also pleased to announce that there will be a surprise for the entire camp. The winner of season thirteen of *RuPaul's Drag Race* is a personal friend of mine, and she has agreed to join our camp drag queens and kings for an Eleganza Extravaganza."

The crowd cheered.

Daniel whispered, "That's Symone. She's from Arkansas, you know."

Nikki shook her head. "I'm behind a few seasons." That was an understatement. She wished she'd watched more, as much of Sunshine Fanta's slang went right over her head.

"She's amazing. I can't wait."

Miranda held a finger to her lips and looked back to the director.

Mr. Novak adjusted the volume of the speaker. "Many of you have friends and family joining us Saturday for the finale of the color tournament, the pinnacle of Camp Iris events, the final Showcase. Everyone is welcome to join us for a buffet beforehand. Now let's get this party started!"

Thomas and the Blue Team marched in carrying a torch while chanting. With much fanfare, he tossed the torch onto the pile of wood. Soon the flames danced.

Gumball whispered in Nikki's ear. "Look. Emily and Tracy are holding hands."

"It's a good idea." Nikki took Gumball's hand.

"They're cute together."

Nikki made a goofy face.

Gumball squeezed her hand. "They are. Not as cute as us, though. Just sayin'. Is she helping Marcus?"

"She said she doesn't do pranks anymore."

"That's a bald lie."

"Says the woman who has tried to out-prank her the entire camp."

Gumball snickered. "So she is helping him."

"I have no idea."

"Only one team can be victorious over the prank war." Gumball scooted closer. "Oh, look, they put colors in the flames."

Nikki shifted her attention. They only had a few days left together. Going home was going to suck.

Chapter Twenty-Eight
August 6

After breakfast, Gumball pulled Nikki outside to a quiet bench. She opened a gumball and popped it in her mouth, then explained her great prank finale. "See, we'll hide their stuff in a closet somewhere and then take empty boxes, cover them with a tarp, and float them in the lake. They'll think we put their stuff out and swim out to get it and nothing will be there."

"I don't know about this one, Gumball. The lake after dark. I'm tired. And we have big competitions coming up. We still have some glitches."

"Have confidence in our team. The robots will work fine. After the Red Team ghillie lake video, we have to up our game. I can't lose."

"I don't think we should do it," Nikki said.

Gumball crossed her arms over her chest. "Either you're with me or against me."

"It seems like a lot of effort." Nikki rubbed her ear.

"It's the finale. Last prank. I promise. Just come on."

"I'm not taking anyone's stuff." Nikki looked around to make sure no one was listening.

Gumball nodded. "Good idea. You go play frisbee golf or something, so everyone will see you and assume we're together. Throw them off our track."

"People assume we're together?"

"We are, literally, together right now." Gumball

smiled.

Nikki flickered a smile back. How together were they? She heard the sprinklers turn on. "Look, in the flower bed."

As the water hit the mulch, a little army of condoms squirmed until they all stood in formation. Gumball took out her phone and snapped a shot. "Just in case it doesn't last."

Nikki laughed. "Who are you sending it to?"

"The entire camp. Including us."

"You're always a step ahead."

"Better than a step behind." Gumball pecked her cheek and was gone.

Nikki's phone chimed. She looked and there was the garden of condoms for everyone at Camp Iris to see.

❧❧❧❧

Later that evening, they stood near the dock. Gumball pulled out a box of supplies. She deftly flipped the cardboard flaps into a box. "Hand me a piece of tape, please."

Nikki pulled off a strip and extended her hand with the dispenser. Gumball pressed her lips together and sealed the carton.

Gumball flipped a canoe and began to stack boxes. "Does that look full enough?"

Nikki nodded. "I guess. Now what?"

"Grab the tarps off the chairs, and I'll use these zip ties to strap them to the canoe seats."

Nikki tugged the blue plastic-coated fabric and flipped it up like she was making a bed. The tarp was too wide, so she crammed the extra fabric into the sides. "Why do you think anyone will look in here?"

"While everyone was at dinner, I went to the gym and took every duffel bag I could find and hid them in a janitor closet."

"You don't think the janitor will notice?"

"Maybe. Maybe not. There's a lot of supplies in there."

"How long until people will think their bags are gone?"

Gumball fussed with a plastic strip. "Sometime in the morning. Until they see the canoes and assume their stuff is in them. They'll have to go out to see."

"Won't they just take another boat?"

"Not if they're all tied together." Gumball grinned.

"Okay, then, how do we get ourselves back to shore?"

"The paddleboat. People don't think outside the box, or in this case, the boat. I'm guessing someone will wade out to see what's going on."

Gumball pulled a shoelace from her pocket and tied a second canoe to the first. "Gah. I shouldn't have quit Girl Scouts so early. How's your knot tying?"

"Right over left, left over right." Nikki scanned the beach for any other campers or staff that might be out.

"That's right. Makes a square knot, tidy and tight." The knot finished, Gumball nudged the tip of the canoe into the water.

They repeated the process for what seemed hours to Nikki. The moon had risen high in the sky, faintly outlining their images against the ground. Once all the canoes were afloat, the tricksters climbed into the paddleboat and nudged the raft farther out into the lake.

Nikki was slowly cycling her feet on the pedals, watching as the mist formed over the water. It was unnervingly still. Even the bugs were quiet. Something startled her and she jumped. She wasn't sure what it was—a fish jumping, maybe. She jerked back and stood.

Gumball hissed, "Sit down."

The boat began to wobble. Nikki waved her arms but couldn't regain her balance. She fell back, pushing the boat away as she dropped out. She yelped as she hit the cool water. She laid her head back and tried to float. Her clothes weighed her down, so she had to tread water but she was able to keep her head above the surface. She tried not to panic as her arms tired. She turned and, in the moonlight, she saw Gumball frantically straining to reach her.

"Hang on. I've almost got you. Try to grab the boat."

Nikki lifted a hand, but the few feet might as well have been a mile. She flailed her arms and kicked with all her strength. She sank down in the water, and she held her breath as long as she could. A pair of hands shoved her up. Nikki gasped and took a big breath. She felt an arm around her and she was dragged through the lake toward the shore. Coughing up water, she was surprised to see Gumball following them in the paddleboat. Who was rescuing her? In the shallow water, Nikki stumbled to her feet.

Emily stood in front of her, still fully dressed and soaking wet. "Are you okay?"

"Emily? You're the one who got me?" Nikki tried to catch her breath.

"Obviously. You seem surprised."

"Well, you know, you sort of hated me."

"I don't actually hate you. And if you knew anything about me at all, you know I would save you." Emily touched Nikki's shoulder. "Serious now, are you okay?"

"Yeah, yeah, I'm alright." Nikki put her hands on her knees, her arms shaking.

Tracy waded in. "Give me your hand."

Nikki did as she was instructed, and Tracy helped her to shore.

Gumball slid the boat into the sand and jumped out. "Thank God you were here. Nikki could have drowned."

Emily said, "No thanks to you, Gumball. What the hell are you two doing out here?"

"It was an accident. I would have jumped in, but you aren't supposed to get in the water to rescue someone."

"Unless you have to." Emily brushed back her wet hair. "Tracy and I were walking, and I heard the splash."

Tracy asked, "Are you sure you're all right? I think I should get a counselor."

Nikki put up a hand. "No need. Thanks to you two, I'm fine. And I'm pretty sure all four of us will get in trouble. Major trouble."

"I agree," Emily said. "If you're sure you're fine. Gumball, these pranks are out of control. We have to stop."

Tracy peered out over the dark water. "Speaking of, what's in the canoes?"

"Boxes," Nikki whispered. "It's supposed to look like people's stuff is in the boats."

Emily put her hands on her hips. "Then they

panic and swim out and it's nothing."

"Something like that." Gumball put an arm around Nikki. "This went really bad."

"I'm fine," Nikki said. "Thanks to Emily."

Emily shrugged. "You'd do the same thing. Let's all just get back to our cabins."

Gumball stuck out her hand. "Thank you. And, great competition this year."

Emily shook her hand. "It's been a lot of fun. This stunt was pretty good, until you tried to drown Nikki."

"Yeah, I didn't count on her jumping around because a fish jumped."

Emily raised an eyebrow. "You could have just pushed them out and let them float away. It's attention to detail where you fail, although I do appreciate your dedication to the craft of pranking."

Gumball slapped Emily on the back. "Just trying to keep up with you. We should hang out more often."

Tracy raised her eyebrows. "Why is she talking about pranks?"

Emily shook her head. "Never mind, I'll explain later. You two have a good night." She took Tracy's hand and they disappeared toward the far side of camp.

Dripping water and shivering, Nikki reached for Gumball's hand as they walked to the cabin. "Seas the day, indeed."

Gumball stopped and turned. "I'm really sorry you fell in. You could have really gotten hurt."

"I never would have thought it would be Emily Morgan who would save me." Nikki quivered.

"I told you she was alright." Gumball put her hands on Nikki's face and gently kissed her. "I'm glad she got you. You know, because I have my good tennis shoes on." She giggled and ran as Nikki chased her.

Chapter Twenty-Nine
August 7

Justin tapped the microphone in the auditorium. "Okay, so today is the flag football tournament. Double elimination. In order to be good sports, the Red Team will challenge a mixed team of Yellow, Blue, Orange and Green. You guys might be able to find eleven people to play from all the teams."

Mr. Novak shooed him from the stage. "Since the Red Team senses an easy victory, let's just have them play each mega team. Let's put together Yellow and Blue, and Orange and Green. Points will be determined by sportsmanship. The team with the most penalties will lose a thousand points." He stared at Justin.

"Oh, yes, this afternoon will be another block of time for your team to practice for the Showcase finale."

Justin yelled, "Try to not hurt yourselves on the field."

"The Red Team is very close to losing to forfeiture." Mr. Novak pointed two of his fingers at his eyes and then at Justin. He turned back to the audience. "Good luck to everyone."

※ ※ ※ ※

Later that morning, Miranda was waiting on the steps when Nikki and Gumball returned from the soccer field. "Let's chat, shall we?"

Gumball winked at Nikki.

Miranda stood and opened the door. "Have a seat in the office."

They each perched on a folding chair.

Gumball folded her hands on her knee. "What's up?"

The counselor leaned on the desk. "There's an interesting situation at the lake this morning. Some of the campers are missing their gear bags, and there are canoes floating around with tarps over piles of stuff. You two seem to have trouble making curfew."

Nikki rubbed her ear, the heat creeping up her neck.

Gumball said, "I didn't realize curfew was mandatory. I thought it was sort of a suggestion."

"Huh." Miranda pushed her glasses up. "Look, most of the pranks were harmless. Funny, but harmless. But this is too far. People are furious. Somehow the band geeks thought their instruments were there, too. They panicked. Their stuff could get ruined."

"Did they just look in the music room?" Gumball said. "I'm sure their instruments are safe. I mean, they're usually careful with expensive equipment. I think they overreacted."

Nikki mumbled, "That's pretty funny. It's just some locker bags missing. No one took instruments that we're aware of."

"You know the drama some people create around themselves." Miranda snickered. "It's kind of funny. But it might smooth things over if they got their stuff back."

Gumball shrugged. "I have no idea. Have they looked in their closets?"

Nikki coughed. "Janitor closet. Cafeteria."

Gumball gave her a warning look.

Miranda waved her hand in front of a rainbow-colored pony. "On a related subject, the counselors compete for best cabin and I won last year. I want to remind you that I am quite fond of this trophy on this shelf. Your shenanigans could cost me."

"I've heard, through rumors of course, that there won't be any more pranks this summer," Gumball said.

Nikki nodded. "I heard there's a truce."

Gumball nudged her. "Camp gossip, but I heard the same thing." She pressed her lips together as if to silence herself.

Miranda studied Gumball's face for a long moment. She folded her arms over her chest. "I hope to win the Color War finale as well. You're sure our robotic dancers are ready for the Showcase?"

Gumball rubbed her fingernails on her chest and blew on them. "I hesitate to brag, you know, because I'm so modest and all. But it's pretty spectacular."

"I had no doubts. But remember you can lose our team points, too, if they catch you."

Gumball winked. "I understand. No worries. I can assure you no more pranks, especially those that may or may not be from anyone on the Yellow Team."

**

After dinner, Nikki stood. "Come on, Einstein. You promised spectacular and we have a few bugs to work out."

Back in the cabin, the friends huddled on Gumball's bunk.

Nikki held up her hand and ticked off each finger as she listed the challenges. "The dancers don't start at the same time, there's two out of sync, one or another stops randomly, and we keep having to reboot—"

"Stop." Gumball glanced around the room.

"Don't let everyone think the Yellow Team is going to lose. I have this."

Nikki crawled to her bunk and looked down as Gumball tapped away at her iPad. Nikki woke with a crick in her neck, the glow of the electronics still shining from Gumball's bunk. Nikki rolled and peered down at Gumball, who stared at the screen.

Nikki slid down. "What's going on?"

Gumball pressed her eyes closed. "I can't fix it. I've tried everything. I failed. What am I going to do?"

Nikki put her hand on Gumball's arm. "What are we going to do…it's we. The team."

"I've let everyone down. I quit."

"Come on, you just need some sleep."

"It's not that. I have tried everything. I might as well go back to square one." She clamped her eyes shut.

Nikki slid down from her bunk. She touched Gumball's cheek, and Gumball opened her eyes.

"We win as a team."

"And we lose as a team," Gumball answered. "I'm sorry." She turned over in her bunk.

Nikki climbed back up to her bed. When the sunlight peeked in under the door, she went to the shower. Standing in the water, she started to sing the first song for the competition robot dance. It was too bad Georgi wasn't here. She would know how to fix it. With a sigh, she turned off the water and leaned her head against the tile. If only Nikki knew how to program. Not only would they fail the competition, even if they were no longer mortal enemies, she was sure Emily Morgan would never let her hear the end of it.

Chapter Thirty
August 8

In the game room, Sam hit a buzzer several times. "Welcome to team *Jeopardy*. We are kicking off with the Yellow Team and Orange Team. Good luck to everyone."

Daniel waved the team into a huddle. "Now listen up. This is supposed to be our time to shine. Relax and go with your first answer. We can tag players in and out, but we can only have four at the table."

Sam spun a wire cage tumbler like they used for bingo. "Inside are these topics which we will select by random spin. Teens on TV, Slanguage, Herstory, Movie Villains, Extreme Geography, Quick Books, Four-Letter Words, University and Colleges, Play Ball, Money Money, Computer, Around the Body, Medieval Times, That's so Cliché, Sounds like it, The Science of It, Flaming Foods, Music Makers, Takes the Prize, All about Pride, and All Hail the Queen."

Daniel swore under his breath. "I suck at geography."

Nikki whispered, "Don't pick me for science or the history stuff."

Asa said, "No math for me. I'm not even to algebra yet."

Miranda pushed her hair behind her ears. "Listen, if they say a category and you think you're good for it, just raise a finger so I can figure out our team."

Sam opened the hinged door and plucked out a

small ball. "Alright, our first category is Four-Letter Words. All the questions will be about a four-letter word. Good luck."

"Shit," Gumball said.

Miranda sighed.

⁂

Nikki held the phone to her ear and strained to listen for her mother's voice over the poor connection.

"Hey, Nik. Is everything okay?"

"Hi, Mom. Yeah, everything is great. I just wanted to remind you that the Showcase is Saturday. They're planning a dinner beforehand in the cafeteria starting at five thirty."

"Ed and I are both excited to see what you've been working on. Do you want us to take you home afterward?"

"Nah, some of us are planning a little party. I should be back at the school by one thirty on Sunday."

**

Nikki lay in her bunk awake, listening to bugs. She opened her eyes when her mattress jabbed her from below.

Gumball said, "Let's go." She slung a backpack on.

Nikki shook her head. "No more pranks."

"It's not. I promise."

"Fine. Camp's almost over. Why should I start sleeping now?" Nikki held Gumball's hand as they wandered through the campus.

As they entered the woods, the canopy of leaves blocked the moonlight. Nikki understood why ancient cultures believed little fairies scurried around the underbrush. Of course, here at camp people had made little houses for them, so maybe not so ancient cultures.

Gumball stopped at a gazebo. She reached up to a post and tiny white lights flickered around the ceiling.

"I didn't even know this was here," Nikki said.

"Well, it's not technically an actual forbidden forest. I found it exploring. I brought a picnic for my lady." She opened her bag and took out several cans of Mountain Dew and Jalapeño Doritos. "I need caffeine, and in hindsight, the spicy chips were a bad choice. I don't have any mints."

"You need to work on attention to detail." Nikki sat on the bench and patted her lap.

Gumball sat down, and Nikki wrapped her arms around her, the softness of her shirt warm against her hands. A month ago, she thought she was a lesbian but was afraid what people would think if they knew. Now, she had a girlfriend and she didn't give a shit what anyone thought. She breathed in the scent of Gumball as she buried her head into Gumball's neck.

Chapter Thirty-One
August 9

The Battle of the Black Death is starting in fifteen minutes. Teams Orange and Blue please report to the field."

Standing on the porch, Nikki would have rather been facing the plague. There was no doubt that the escape room was a real haunted house. The windows were covered with so much dirt you couldn't see through them. Spider webs hung from the railing, and though they were fake, it was creepy even in the daylight. She swallowed down her nausea, her palms sweaty and cold. There was no way to know how the other houses had done, but this was an opportunity to stack on a pile of points. They were the smartest kids at the camp, maybe, besides the political junkies. Nikki looked at her teammates and opened the door. Daniel had painted his nails neon yellow for the event and bravely went first. Miranda followed him in her yellow coveralls. Gumball, McKenzie, Aaron, Elliot, Hunter, Jesse, and Asa all crammed into the darkened lobby with Nikki.

It might all come down to the points for the Showcase, and Nikki predicted they would win. The robots were awesome. Gumball had figured out the glitch, and the dance number was killer. Gumball shifted next to her, their hands barely touching. A heat began to rise in Nikki's chest.

Thunder echoed from speakers across the

ceiling, followed by maniacal laughter. Three doors appeared under spotlights. Witches and Warlocks, Ancient Egypt, Gay Paris.

Miranda whispered, "I'm not good at French."

Gumball snickered. "That's not what I heard."

Nikki jabbed her with an elbow. "Ancient Egypt, then."

Painted like a sarcophagus, the doorknob was disguised. The crew leaned close to examine the frame when it opened.

A small screen on the table flickered on, and the image of Mr. Novak wearing a pith helmet came into focus. "Greetings. I beg of you to assist me. I have begun to inventory the items collected from the last expedition, and the special treasure is missing. I'm afraid it's the key to solving the mystery of the death of the king. Until we find the tomb, it's anyone's guess how this item relates to the possible murder. Thank you for risking potential death during the search. You may discover snakes, scorpions, traps left by the builders, or even a deadly curse. Securing the treasure is vital. You must find it before my traitorous assistant sells it on the black market and the true history is lost forever. I must go. Someone is coming."

The screen went dark.

A voice spoke from a small speaker. "Welcome, explorers. Once you enter the chamber, you will have one hour to solve the riddles. Find the clues to the treasure and solve the mystery of the death of the king, or spend eternity with the deceased." There was a pause. "Not really. If you get stuck at a puzzle for more than five minutes, I'll ring the phone and give you a clue. Cheers."

Gumball shrugged, then pushed on the door

before them. Nikki stepped forward, her shoe sliding on the sand. The light on the ceiling was yellow, giving an odd pallor to her fellow explorers. Painted on large sheets of paper, hieroglyphics covered the walls. The room was empty except for a small desk with assorted office supplies, and most peculiarly, children's wooden alphabet blocks scattered across the cover of a notebook.

Miranda tapped the journal and said, "This is obviously the first clue."

"Open it," Nikki said.

There was a compartment inside the pages. "It's pieces of a puzzle," Miranda announced.

Daniel took charge. "Gumball, help me with the puzzle. The rest of you look over everything on the desk. Under it, everywhere."

Aaron held up a pair of scissors pinned closed with a padlock. "And maybe we need these later?"

Nikki carefully scanned the items in the room.

Jesse picked up a block. "Who's good at *Wheel of Fortune*?"

"You and Nikki figure that out," Miranda said. "Gumball and Daniel almost have the picture finished."

"It's a map," Gumball said. "With a pyramid with chambers marked off, except one."

Aaron asked, "Does anyone see any numbers?"

"Keep looking around." Miranda leaned toward the team working out the word clue.

"Wait, how many numbers?" Asa asked.

Hunter pushed up their glasses. "Total of four digits."

After spelling out *planet, petal, heptane,* and *eaten,* Nikki and Jesse agreed it must be *elephant.*

Jesse held up a hand. "Stop a minute. Everyone

look at the walls. Find an elephant. Should stick out with the other symbols."

Nikki moved close to the paper and studied the marks.

Daniel tapped the wall. "I got it. And underneath are tiny numbers."

"There's a magnifying glass in the cup." Miranda picked it up and peered in. "Try one two three four. Honestly. I could have guessed that."

Aaron flushed as he worked the tumblers. He shouted, "I got the lock off!"

Miranda held a finger toward the wall. "Good, because there's a string here."

With much fanfare, Aaron snipped. A window shade rolled up, exposing a small three-by-three-foot square opening to the next room.

"Good thing I skipped the extra pie at lunch." Daniel shrugged, bits of glitter dropping off his shirt as he leaned forward to crawl through.

When all of them made it inside, they could barely move. Shelves went from floor to ceiling on one wall, stacked with dolls and boxes.

"Anyone claustrophobic?" Miranda asked. "Besides me, I mean."

McKenzie said, "Let's hurry. What are those boxes?"

Asa squealed. "Candy boxes. Look, there's a paper on the desk. Almond, nugget, coconut cream. Candy. Aaron, you still have the scissors? Maybe cut the dotted lines."

Gumball counted the shapes. "Okay, we're looking for a candy box with thirteen shapes on the lid."

Daniel asked, "Who the hell made all this stuff?

Honestly. This is like a preschooler made them."

"You didn't think everyone went to Potion Bottle Decorating class?" Aaron laughed.

McKenzie shrugged. "I didn't. Never mind. I found the box."

"I did too," both Nikki and Daniel said.

"Match up the papers." Miranda swiped them around.

Some papers matched on all three, some only one. Daniel moved a paper between two.

Nikki said, "Stop. We have to go one piece at a time. As soon as one doesn't fit, that box is eliminated."

"It's this one." Aaron pointed.

"Open it."

"It says, 'Don't watch the clock. Do what it does. Keep going.'"

"Go where? Is anything ticking?" Asa swiveled his head.

Miranda put her hands on her hips. "Are you kidding me? Just look for clocks. Who can read a non-digital clock?"

They all answered, "I can."

"Just checking."

Hunter said, "Hey, did you notice they all say eleven thirty?"

"Is there a padlock on anything? Try one one three zero," Aaron said as he sifted through the nearest shelf.

Nikki said, "There's a latch and a lock on this box."

"Got it." Gumball twirled the numbers. "Only it's not opening."

"Let me try." Daniel slowly twisted each tumbler. "Nope."

The phone rang. Hunter lifted the receiver. "Yes?"

"Sorry, that lock keeps sticking. Give it yank."

Hunter said, "He said give it a yank."

McKenzie jerked the lock and the barrier popped open. They tipped out strips of paper. "You have got to be kidding me. The next clue went through a shredder."

Gumball grabbed some. "Everybody take a few."

For several moments they each tried to read the lettering. Jesse figured out the hint. "Just take the pink papers. There's fewer of those."

Nikki wiped sweat from her forehead. "Look, this one has a tiny number at the bottom. Who's got one?"

"Lay them on this shelf, in order," Miranda said as she lined up a strip. "Here's two."

Aaron held up a tape dispenser. Gumball poked him. "Office supplies your specialty?"

He pulled off a piece with a snap. "I have many talents."

They snickered.

With a few adjustments, the paper lined up. The sheet was cryptic.

Gumball said, "Hieroglyphics. I heart bugs. Two bugs. I heart two bugs."

"They're beetles," Miranda said.

Daniel said, "Wait, I found a box with CDs in it. Maybe there's one from The Beatles."

"Elton John, Queen, Violent Femmes, Indigo Girls. Who picked these out?" Miranda pointed. "There it is. The Beatles. White Album. Open it."

"It's all in hieroglyphics," Daniel said. "We need a decoder."

"I found a board with decoders on it. But there's four," Nikki said.

"Line them so they match. The eye of Ra goes with three o'clock on this one and nine on that one." Gumball looked at Nikki, who had her mouth open. "What? I know more than computers."

Nikki winked. She twisted the dial. "Okay, let's see, the first letter is X. Then M. Someone write this down."

Asa grabbed a crayon and scribbled each letter. Then he read, "X marks the spot. Solve for X."

Hunter asked, "Then each clue tells you where you are?"

Gumball scanned the paper. "No. Solve for X to find your way forward. It's a clue."

"What the hell does that mean?" Daniel said.

"Where's the map?" Miranda asked. "Look on the back."

Jesse poked Daniel. "Come on, it's a math problem. You're up."

"I don't have a pencil," he protested.

"Asa does, but you can probably solve it out loud."

"Fine." Daniel crossed his arms.

Jesse read, "Start with prime and you'll be fine."

"Obvious." Daniel smirked. "One times two times three times five equals thirty."

"Uh-oh." Jesse looked at Asa. "Give him the crayon and find a paper."

$6x + 33 - 2(3x + 1)$

Daniel scribbled. "It's thirty-one. Numbers in a series? What the hell does that mean?"

"It tells us where we are, right. X marks the spot," Gumball said.

Miranda said, "Flip over the map. Anyone see anything?"

Several minutes passed. Miranda said, "Are there coordinates on the map?"

The phone rang. "You are getting warm."

Daniel brushed the sweat from his forehead. "What the hell? Of course we're warm. We're in Egypt, right?"

"No, he means we're getting close to solving it," Nikki said. "Look at the map again."

Hunter sighed. "Nothing. There are no numbers."

Aaron said, "Wait, this picture on the wall is a map, too. And it has longitude and latitude lines on it. And there's a lever on the bottom of the frame." He pushed it. It clicked as it moved and the wall shifted.

"It's another door!" Gumball said.

They went into the opening the size of a closet and found themselves pushing through clothes into a small sitting room.

Daniel said, "Check the sofa and that chair. Look in the umbrella stand."

Nikki went back to look in the closet. Explorer shirts hung with a pith hat on the shelf. Boots sat on the floor.

Gumball touched her shoulder. "Start with the boots, and I'll look in the hat."

"There's nothing."

The phone rang. "Keep it safe from pickpockets."

Gumball said, "Look in the pockets."

"Shit, there must be a dozen shirts. Start looking for one with an inside pocket."

"I got it." A scrap of paper said, "Say cheese."

They looked wildly around the room. "Anyone see a camera?"

Asa said, "Or a mouse? Maybe it's not that tricky."

They all stared at him.

He said, "We have to think outside the box."

"I don't think so," Miranda said. "Look in the trunk."

"It's empty."

Gumball pointed to the wall. "Hey, the head on the sphinx is RuPaul."

Nikki touched a frame. "Between those two explorers is a mummy smiling."

"Weird, because you can't really see the face that well, normally."

Miranda smacked her forehead. "Come on people, think."

Hunter pointed. "The only unaltered picture is that dude over the mantel."

Gumball pushed on the frame and it swung away from the wall. "Great. A safe."

"I've had it with this." Miranda sat on the couch.

Aaron said, "Don't give up now."

"It's a vase." Gumball took it down. "There's a plastic knife inside."

Daniel smiled. "And it's been bedazzled."

The lights went on high and another panel opened. A recording announced, "You have found the treasure and solved the death of the king."

Nikki said, "What? How does that solve the murder?"

"Oh, I don't care," Miranda said. "Let's get out of here."

On the way down the steps, Gumball took Nikki's hand. "Wait a minute." Her face was drawn and pale.

Nikki called out, "Hey, y'all go on. We'll catch up."

Gumball scuffed the toe of her shoe at the ground.

After the others had left, Nikki asked, "What's up?"

Gumball stared at her fingernails. "I have a surprise. Well, not a surprise, a thing. I'm doing a thing."

Nikki waited.

Gumball sputtered, "I signed up to do the drag show."

Nikki squeezed her hands. "And you're nervous?"

"I thought maybe you'd think it was weird."

"We programmed robots to dance. That's weird. I'm proud of you. Trying something new."

Gumball bent over. "I might vomit."

Nikki patted her back. "You'll be great. Just take a slow breath."

That afternoon, the Orange Team and the Yellow Team were in a heated game of Pictionary. The points spread between them was slight, and this might give an edge if they could win.

Daniel said, "This is the final card. Come on. For the victory."

Nikki drew a card for "couple" and groaned. She began to scribble two stick figures.

Gumball yelled, "Mom and Dad."

Nikki looked at her. At a camp soaked with all things rainbow related, Gumball thought of parents. She considered putting boobs on them, but instead she drew two birds.

"Flock."

Nikki tapped the paper.

"Noah's ark."

Nikki put her hands up in the air. Finally, she grabbed Gumball and kissed her. The timer rang.

Gumball said, "Great. We just lost."

"Did we?" Nikki kissed her again.

Chapter Thirty-Two
August 10

The Battle of the Black Death is starting in fifteen minutes. Teams Yellow, Red, and Green report to the field."

At the soccer pitch, Thomas handed a foam noodle to each person. "Remember, you have to pull back on the strike so you don't hurt someone. This is an honor system, so die when you're killed. Overzealous bopping will result in ejection from the game."

Nikki glared at the Red Team.

"Listen up, people. This game is one of two final challenges for points, winning team takes all. To start with, everyone is a peasant in the Middle Ages, costumes optional." Thomas laughed to himself. "Some peasants are zombies, and one peasant is the necromancer, the practitioner of the black magic of death. Once we start the battle, anyone who is deemed killed must fall to the ground, and the secret necromancer can touch them and they become a zombie."

Hunter said, "So a zombie can get killed and then be turned back into a zombie? Cool."

"Yeah, cool," Nikki mumbled.

"Now, if a peasant figures out who the necromancer is and kills him, her, or them, all the zombies die and the peasants will win. If all the peasants are converted, the necromancer and the zombies win. Points go with each player toward their team score, plus bonus points I might award for outstanding performance."

Daniel put a hand to his heart, staggered, and fell to the ground.

"Yes. Like that." Thomas bowed to Daniel. "Okay, everyone count off to five, and every fifth person is a zombie."

Nikki looked at the brace on her wrist. "Gumball, I don't think…"

"Just count off."

"Fine. Four."

"We're both peasants anyway."

"All the zombies over here. Peasants, on this side. Each peasant should draw a paper, read it, and then put it in this other bag. Don't say what it says."

Nikki took her paper. It was blank.

Gumball whispered, "It's not me."

"Good." The two stared across the gathering crowd of peasants, hoping for a clue to the necromancer. "Let's make sure we watch the ground to see if we find someone raising the dead."

Nikki sighed. "I need more sunscreen."

The whistle blew and some of the students began to stagger around the field, waving their colorful weapons.

Gumball yelled and ran toward the zombies.

Nikki gripped her noodle, the plastic slipping under her sweaty touch. Who would have thought the lightsaber class would have been a better choice than archery for not one, but two events? She took a deep breath, the summer air still and humid. The moans from the zombies drowned out the harp music playing in the background. As she stepped forward, a yell behind her matched a sudden pain on the back of her head. The world fell away into darkness as she dropped to the ground.

Voices around her were indecipherable as Nikki sensed the white lights over her. The coolness behind her neck contrasted the heat of a blanket. She pushed at the fabric.

"There she is. How're you feeling, Nikki?" Stephanie asked.

"Where am I?"

"On the field. You had a run-in with a super zealous zombie, I'm afraid."

"Who was it?"

"I'm not sure. Other than a good bop on the head, you seem to be okay. I don't really have a concussion protocol, but I'm thinking I need to add one. I'm afraid you're done with physical challenges for a few days."

Nikki said, "All we have left is the Showcase tomorrow. How long do I have to rest?"

McKenzie leaned down. "I hate to be an ass, but we had to stop the game. Can you get up?"

Stephanie held up a hand. "I'd like the doc to take a quick peek."

"I'm fine, really. I'm just going to walk back to our cabin. Honest." Nikki sat up on the grass. She reached for the hands around her. "I'm good. Hey, you guys kill them, eh?"

Nikki shuffled to the dorm and climbed into her bed. She covered her eyes with an arm and thought of all the things she loved about camp besides Gumball. She had just dozed off when her team burst into the room.

Daniel waved his arms as he spoke. "It was great, I was the necromancer, and no one figured it out until almost the end. Gumball killed me and we all win!"

"With bonus points for killing a cabin mate, I might add." Gumball beamed. "We beat the Red Team.

Halleloo!"

※ ※ ※ ※

Nikki strained to breathe in the stuffy dressing room. Bright lights over mirrors lit up the makeup scattered on the counter. The thump from the bass rumbled in as an old disco tune played on the stage to their left.

Nikki spoke through the door to a bathroom stall. "You don't have to do this."

Gumball slowly opened the door. She had on jeans with a black T-shirt and a leather vest. Her hair was hidden under a leather baseball cap and a mascara mustache gave at least the hint of masculinity. "I can't go on. This makeup is the worst."

"Camp is supposed to be about being free to explore, including the lines of gender." She leaned in to kiss Gumball.

"No, my mustache." Gumball jumped back. "Fine. I'm going out. But if anyone laughs…"

"No one will laugh. Mr. Novak would deduct a hundred points on the spot."

Gumball took a deep breath. "Actually, Sunshine Fanta might take a thousand."

Nikki smiled and patted Gumball. "Right. I'm not allowed in the waiting area, so you go on. I'll be watching from the front row."

Nikki had just taken her seat when the first notes of "We're Not Going to Take It" by Twisted Sister began. Gumball strutted onto the stage.

As Nikki predicted, the crowd cheered and joined the dance. Gumball worked the room like the only rooster in a crowded henhouse.

Chapter Thirty-Three
August 11

Mr. Novak snapped his fingers and the room quieted. "This morning we have a special presentation for our camp meeting. Trust me, you'll have plenty of time for any final touch-ups on your Showcase presentations. Please put your hands together for 'Queer Eye for the Counselor Guy.'"

A picture of Marcus appeared on the screen, his polo shirt hanging over cutoff shorts. Daniel and Sam from the Green Team sauntered onto the stage.

Daniel said, "I am quite relieved we didn't have to approach habitat and feeding rituals, as I'm sure teaching these people to clean and cook would have put me in my grave."

Mr. Novak cleared his throat.

Daniel continued. "Sam and I had a team work with wardrobe and—ahem—personal hygiene."

The campers snickered.

Sam waved a hand. "As you can see, underneath that schlumpy exterior, a budding dapper dresser is quite hidden."

Marcus strolled on stage, paused at the center, turned, walked to the front, and posed with a hand on his hip. The crowd clapped and stomped. His hair had been styled, and he was clean shaven. He wore long pants with a pair of boat shoes, and a buttoned shirt hung open at the neckline. He waved and retreated backstage.

A giant image of Thomas wearing running shorts and a tank top with boots appeared on the screen. The logo on his shirt said, "I'm a fermata. Hold me." He had shaved his beard, such as it was, but his hair hung over his eyes and curled over his ears.

Daniel said, "While I give props to the boots, this, folks, is the definition of a hot mess."

Thomas strode out still wearing his boots, but with coveralls and a flannel shirt.

Sam said, "If the trees aren't scared around here…"

The campers clapped and whistled.

Justin appeared on the slide show, his biceps flexing in his image. The basketball uniform didn't seem that bad to Nikki.

Justin poked his head out from behind the curtain. "Are you ready?"

The crowd cheered.

He strolled out in khakis and a suit coat, his brown saddle shoes making a statement.

Mr. Novak clapped as he approached. "Let's have all our models back on stage. I'd say they were good sports, and I can assure you that clothes make the man."

A picture of the three participants in dresses popped up. The crowd went nuts.

**

Classical music swelled from the speakers as the patrons filled the seats of the auditorium. The large screen over the stage glowed with images from the time at camp. Everyone had a phone and there were dozens and dozens of pictures flipping every few seconds.

At seven sharp, Mr. Novak approached the podium at the side of the stage. The music faded but the pictures continued. "Welcome, distinguished guests, friends and family, and campers. You may have noticed the team banners and posters around the auditorium this evening. Our students are grouped by musical ability, the arts and acting, dance and movement, computer sciences, and political/social media influencers. For the past four weeks, campers have participated in classes and created crafts as well as completed preparation for the team tournament. They competed in events requiring physical strength and coordination, mental challenges and problem solving, and most importantly, it required cooperation and creative thinking."

As if on cue, the image of Sunshine Fanta and the performers from drag night appeared above him and froze.

He waved an arm toward the screen. "We all enjoyed the opportunity to explore our identities and celebrate our individuality in a safe environment."

The screen went dark.

"Tonight's Showcase is the culminating final contest where our teams demonstrate their amazing abilities. These presentations are worth the most points and can tip the Color War in favor of any team. We are very proud of their efforts, and I know you will enjoy the show."

❧ ❧ ❧ ❧

Nikki spotted her mom in the audience. She expected Ed but was surprised to see Casey as well.

Her stomach rolled. Gumball was still tweaking the programming an hour ago. They hadn't tested the entire show. The Red Team was next and waiting along the wall in the hallway. When the show started, the Yellow Team snuck to the side of the stage to watch. Thumping dance music started, and the Red Team made the most of the strength and athleticism of their members while completing a complicated dance. When they finished their combination dance/ tumbling routine, Nikki followed the Yellow Team to the orchestra pit and they each took a controller. Most of them weren't doing anything, but it appeared to be a team effort that way.

Right on cue, McKenzie flew her drone over the heads of the audience. Jazz music started and the drone buzzed down to the stage. As it moved from left to right, a robot followed it on stage.

Nikki heard someone say, "Even my Roomba can do that."

To her surprise, Emily held up a fist. "Stop. It's cool. Shut up and watch."

Nikki indeed had misjudged her. She enthusiastically tapped on her game controller, knowing the software running the robots was independent. Asa grinned and waved to someone in the audience. She nudged him. "Remember, we have to act like we're running things."

The robot began to step from side to side, swinging its arm down, then closed its hand as if snapping to the music. The counselors sitting in the wings looked at each other and smiled. A second robot hopped out and joined the first, then a third, then the fourth. The music changed to a country reel with violins. They faced each other like a square dance, bowed, then did a do-si-do.

A robot voice said, "Roll Away To A Half Sashay."

The robots made a circle and held hands.

"Promenade."

The audience clapped as four more robots walked out on the stage and lined up behind them. Bells chimes echoed in the room. They all raised their arms, then one leg like a ninja crane pose.

Someone in the audience gave a yell. "Wax on, wax off."

Another voice said, "Shut up, Harold. Watch the show."

The song changed to an old rock song and they rotated to do the twist. Campers stood and began to dance along. Soon, the music morphed into a calypso beat and the robots formed a single row and started a conga line: step, step, kick. As they completed the ring around the stage, they spun and waved their arms to dance the mashed potato. A robot dog scampered onto the stage and the music changed to a steady, thumping dance beat. The audience clapped along. As the dog started to do a kick pattern, the other robots clapped and then joined in the steps. The dog bowed and then jumped, all four feet in the air. It ran off stage and the robots all lined up front to back. Bollywood music rang through the auditorium and the robots looked at the ceiling as if searching for the source of the sound. They moved behind the first robot so only the one was visible. They raised their arms so it appeared like the Hindu goddess Durga, each following the movement of the first robot. The sound of a giant bell rang out and a cancan blasted from the speakers. The little robots ran in tempo to form a front line, touched elbows, and began to do kicks like the old-time music hall dancers. They bowed in series, and then froze. Most of the audience didn't notice the other drones flying toward the stage until the last moment, when a few people pointed toward them. With a pop, rainbow confetti shot down onto the crowd. The music stopped. The robots patted each other on the back, waved to the audience, and walked off stage.

The audience leaped to its feet, clapping and cheering, the paper still floating in the air.

Nikki hugged Gumball. "You did it! I knew you could. That was awesome!"

**

At the refreshment table, Nikki's family caught up to her.

Her mom pulled her into a hug. "What a wonderful show. How did you get those toys to dance? It was wonderful."

"Honey, they're robots, not toys," Ed said. "And it was amazing. The whole show was just great."

Casey snapped her gum. "The drones were cool. Especially the confetti. Do you think you could do that at the football games?"

Nikki grinned. "We aren't technically supposed to fly them over people, but I'm sure we can figure something out."

Chapter Thirty-Four
August 12

The luggage piled on the porch signaled that the moment Nikki dreaded was here. Home was like a distant memory, standing here at camp in the shade. It was like it didn't even exist anymore. In just a few moments, camp wouldn't exist. She had her first girlfriend, and now they would be apart.

Nikki stood awkwardly, Gumball's hand in hers. Her throat was tight. "I was nervous to come to Camp Iris, and now I don't want to go home." Tears welled in her eyes.

Gumball touched her cheek. "I'm so glad I met you. And we have texts, video chats, and I can make you videos of my cat in costumes when I get home."

Nikki's eyebrows shot up. "You put your cat in costumes?"

"No, I just said that to make you laugh." Gumball moved closer. "I like it when you smile."

Nikki kissed her. "I like this better."

"Look, it's not like we won't ever see each other. Maybe you'll get into Tech and we can room together."

"Maybe?"

Gumball snickered. "Yeah, they probably have a communications program or something."

Nikki punched her arm. "You don't think I can do engineering?"

Gumball kissed her cheek. "I have no doubt."

Nikki swiped at her eyes. "I'm going to miss you."

"I'm glad. I'd hate to have to hunt around for a new girlfriend next camp."

The air brakes of the buses announced their arrival. Nikki sagged as her bravado faded. Gumball pressed something into her hand.

"Don't look until you get on the bus." With that, Gumball grabbed her bags and headed toward the farthest bus.

Nikki slung her gear toward the bin, adjusted her backpack strap, and then found a seat.

"Gamer girl," Emily mumbled as she walked past Nikki.

"See you, Emily."

Emily turned around. "Glad you were at camp, nerd."

Nikki looked up. "Really?"

"Not that much. Some. Don't make it all weird when we get to school."

Nikki opened the paper Gumball had given her. She expected some slightly romantic thing. Instead, it read:

Dear Gumball,

For the best pranks ever at Camp Iris, I award the Yellow Team a hundred points.

For not getting caught, I award you a thousand.

—Mr. Novak.

Her phone pinged. *No more kissing of frogs, I found my princess.*

That was more like it.

Chapter Thirty-Five
August 19

Nikki twirled the colored string bracelet between her fingers, the basement room dark with just a hint of light at the window curtain.

Georgi called out as she skipped down the steps, "Hey, you ready for a slaying?"

Nikki smiled as Georgi plopped next to her. Nikki handed her the friendship bracelet. "You know I like you more than my dice collection."

Georgi tied the bracelet on her wrist. "I like you more than my goldfish."

Nikki picked at a fingernail. "You don't mind if we add someone to our team? Just for today?"

Georgi turned to Nikki. "As long as it's the new girlfriend, no, of course not. Any time."

Nikki pushed a couple buttons on the controller. On screen, her avatar shifted into motion. Georgi's green-haired character moved into view. She adjusted her headset and said, "It's all good, Gumball."

An electronic figure exploded from the shadows, a hot pink battle suit with a matching pink mohawk. The avatar flashed a peace sign.

Georgi snickered. "I think we're all going to get along just fine."

Gumball's avatar did a low bow. "Greetings, best friend of Nikki. I, too, have a surprise. Can I add a player?"

Georgi looked at Nikki.

Nikki said, "Um, I guess."

Gumball's avatar waved an arm. "It's someone you know." An avatar in a rainbow basketball uniform popped on the screen.

"You invited Emily?" Nikki said.

Emily said, "I'm not very good, but I'm a quick learner. Shall we go kick some butt?"

"Yeah, I think we're all friends." Gumball snapped her gum. "Is that cool?"

Georgi said, "Fine by me, as long as no one shoots me from our own team."

Emily and Gumball both said, "Nikki!"

Nikki laughed. "Let's go kick butt."

If you liked this book...

Share a review with your friends or post a review on your favorite site like Amazon, Goodreads, Barnes and Noble, or anywhere you purchased the book. Or perhaps share a posting on your social media sites and help spread the word.

Join the Sapphire Newsletter and keep up with all your favorite authors.

Did we mention you get a free book for joining our team?

sign-up at - www.sapphirebooks.com

About the author

McGee Mathews won the 2019 Lesfic Bard Award for new author. She is a member of the Golden Crown Literary Society, Rainbow Romance Writers and, formerly, the Romance Writers of America.

Check out McGee's other book

You Can't Outrun Your Roots – ISBN – 978-1-952270-82-6

What if instead of meeting someone new, you reconnected with someone from your past?

As Southern as fried chicken and peach cobbler, free spirit Gloria Robinson spent her lifetime building a successful permaculture farm on the tired dirt of former cotton fields in South Carolina. Now widowed, Gloria is certain she'll never find someone new, not in this town. She wouldn't even know how to try. Politically, she fears her years of effort for social justice are slipping backward. She's becoming weary, but she's digging in her heels.

Living in Washington D.C., perpetually single, party girl Anna May Walker floats through life disconnected from her roots in the South. Self-focused, she often ponders how she wronged Gloria in high school. When Anna May's father dies, she heads home to lure her mother to move near her in a retirement community.

Avoiding each other in a small town is impossible, particularly when Anna May's boss unwittingly assigns her to write a story about Gloria's farm. After decades apart, will the old sparks be enough to restart a fire between them?

Keeping Secrets – ISBN – 978-1-952270-04-8

What would you do if, after finally finding the woman

of your dreams, she suddenly leaves to fight in the Civil War?

It's 1863, and Elizabeth Hepscott has resigned herself to a life of monotonous boredom far from the battlefields as the wife of a Missouri rancher. Her fate changes when she travels with her brother to Kentucky to help him join the Union Army. On a whim, she poses as his little brother and is bullied into enlisting, as well. Reluctantly pulled into a new destiny, a lark decision quickly cascades into mortal danger.

While Elizabeth's life has made a drastic U-turn, Charlie Schweicher, heiress to a glass-making fortune, is still searching for the only thing money can't buy.

A chance encounter drastically changes everything for both of them. Will Charlie find the love she's longed for, or will the war take it all away?

Slaying Dragons - 978-1-952270-67-3

Dani Powell's life had been a series of extreme highs and the devastating lows. Medications and the therapy sessions keep her centered on her art, music, and painting. All a reflection of where her mind is at that moment in time. As she struggles to keep the chaos at bay her partner Andrea Fenwick is her safe port in a stormy ocean

Andrea Fenwick juggles a busy accounting job while trying to keep her partner Dani grounded. Their lives together have had their ups and downs, but Andrea never expect the downs to be rock bottom. She'd determined to keep Dani afloat even if it means her best may not be good enough this time.

Tommie Andrews, a computer whiz and occasional dog trainer, discovers she's developing a crush on her friend and co-worker Andrea. The more she tries to be supportive of Andrea,
the more apparent it becomes that friendship may be the most she can hope for. The timing couldn't be worse. Or could it?

When will things get better for the three women? First, they must define "better."

Other books by Sapphire Authors

Dusty Road Home - 978-1-952270-72-7

Melanie Crenshaw has fallen off the proverbial map. Notoriously private on a good day, the world-famous mystery author has gone dark to avoid any public blowback or scandal from her latest failed relationship. Seeking quiet and solace, she retreats to her rural hometown, hoping isolation will be just the atmosphere she needs to finish her novel. But going back home is never as easy as it sounds, especially when a nosy reporter starts sniffing around.

Pulitzer-winning investigative journalist Pilar Stein has seen people at their worst—and has the scars to prove it. After taking time off to heal from a particularly brutal assignment, she's back in the saddle and ready to reclaim her place among the elite of hard-hitting reporters. Unfortunately, her re-entry story—a profile on elusive author Melanie Crenshaw who has suddenly disappeared—seems to lack the teeth necessary to catapult her back to the top of her game.

Appearances are deceiving, of course, and Pilar soon discovers that what she deems a simple fluff piece might well lead to the scoop of a generation…just not the one she expected.

As Melanie fights to maintain her privacy while Pilar takes a backhoe to her past, the two women find themselves torn between their own professional convictions and their growing attraction to each other.

And no matter which road they take, it's going to be a bumpy ride.

Betrayal (As We Know It Book 3) - 978-1-952270-69-7

Betrayal is the exciting conclusion to the As We Know It series.

The survivors at Whitaker Estate are still reeling from the vicious attack on their community, which left three of their friends dead.

When the mysterious newcomer Alaina Renato reveals there is a traitor in their midst, it threatens to tear the community apart. Is there truly a traitor, or is Alaina playing them all?

Dillon Mitchell and the other Commission members realize their group might not survive another attack, especially if there is someone working against them from the inside. Despite the potential risk, they vote to attend a summit that will bring together other survivors from around the country.

When the groups converge on Las Vegas, the festive atmosphere soon turns somber upon the discovery of an ominous threat. But is the danger coming from within, or is there someone else lurking in the city?

Before it's too late, they must race against time to determine where the betrayal is coming from.